T5-DHJ-213

From the Case Files of Shelby Woo

THE CRIME: Someone's mugging Cocoa Beach tourists, and Shelby's favorite hangout, C.J.'s, is the focus of the investigation.

THE QUESTION: Did Will do it—or was he framed?

THE SUSPECTS: *Will*—Shelby's friend, found leaning over the third mugging victim. A lack of an alibi and new evidence don't help his case.

Linda—the new waitress at C.J.'s. Muggings began the same night she started working at C.J.'s, the night she was late arriving home.

Jason—artist and night manager at C.J.'s, desperate for money to pay a loan shark—or pay the price!

Cory—teenage loan shark with a hot new sports car; seen at C.J.'s the nights of all three muggings.

COMPLICATIONS: All clues lead to Will—but Shelby pursues all the suspects, nearly colliding with her boss, Detective Hineline, who warns her off the case.

The Mystery Files of Shelby Woo™

#1 A Slash in the Night
#2 Takeout Stakeout

Available from MINSTREL Books

For orders other than by individual consumers, Pocket Books grants a discount on the purchase of **10 or more** copies of single titles for special markets or premium use. For further details, please write to the Vice-President of Special Markets, Pocket Books, 1633 Broadway, New York, NY 10019-6785, 8th Floor.

For information on how individual consumers can place orders, please write to Mail Order Department, Simon & Schuster Inc., 200 Old Tappan Road, Old Tappan, NJ 07675.

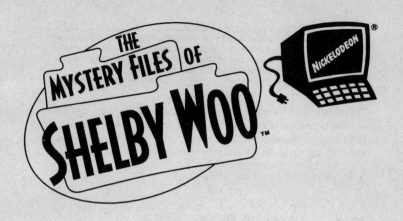

TAKEOUT STAKEOUT

DIANA G. GALLAGHER

Published by POCKET BOOKS

New York   London   Toronto   Sydney   Tokyo   Singapore

The sale of this book without its cover is unauthorized. If you purchased this book without a cover, you should be aware that it was reported to the publisher as "unsold and destroyed." Neither the author nor the publisher has received payment for the sale of this "stripped book."

This book is a work of fiction. Names, characters, places and incidents are products of the author's imagination or are used fictitiously. Any resemblance to actual events or locales or persons, living or dead, is entirely coincidental.

A MINSTREL PAPERBACK *Original*

 A Minstrel Book published by
POCKET BOOKS, a division of Simon & Schuster Inc.
1230 Avenue of the Americas, New York, NY 10020

Copyright © 1997 by Viacom International Inc. All rights reserved. Based on the Nickelodeon series entitled "The Mystery Files of Shelby Woo"

All rights reserved, including the right to reproduce this book or portions thereof in any form whatsoever. For information address Pocket Books, 1230 Avenue of the Americas, New York, NY 10020

ISBN: 0-671-01152-9

First Minstrel Books printing July 1997

10 9 8 7 6 5 4 3 2 1

NICKELODEON and all related titles, logos, and characters are trademarks of Viacom International inc.

A MINSTREL BOOK and colophon are registered trademarks of Simon & Schuster Inc.

Cover photography by Jeffery Salter and Tom Hurst

Printed in the U.S.A.

With love and affection
for my sister, Wendy Sands,
the only member of the family
with detective experience.

Chapter
1

Shelby Woo blinked as Detective Whit Hineline tossed a Cocoa Beach Police badge on her desk. "What's this?" she asked.

"My badge. Polish it." The detective never broke stride as he moved on to his own desk.

"Sure. No problem." Sighing, Shelby stared wistfully at the tarnished metal shield. Fascinated by the cases her grandfather, Mike Woo, had solved when he worked with the San Francisco Police Department as a criminalist, she had dreamed of becoming a real detective with her own badge for years. Part of that dream had been realized when her parents decided she should leave China to go to school in Florida. Now she lived with her retired grandfather at his

1

bed-and-breakfast, the Easterly Breeze. He had helped her get a part-time job at the Cocoa Beach Police Department, but even though she had solved several crimes, no one at the station took her seriously.

But one of these days . . . A mischievous grin brightened Shelby's face as she rummaged through her desk drawer for a polishing cloth. She didn't need a badge to be a detective. She just had to be very careful that no one caught her investigating—especially Detective Hineline and her grandfather. Shelby simply couldn't resist a good mystery, and she never let *anything* discourage her until a case was solved.

And in her present case, Shelby reflected soberly, she was even more determined than usual to track down the truth. The primary suspect was a close friend.

Frowning, Shelby set Hineline's badge aside, clicked open her computer, and started tapping away on the keyboard.

The tourist robberies aren't the most shocking crimes we've ever had in Cocoa Beach, but this is a sunny little resort town. People come here to get away from winter weather and to have a good time. They don't expect anything bad to happen to ruin their vacations. But someone is making a habit of holding up tourists late at night. As you can imagine, the mayor was getting pretty upset because the police didn't have any leads. Until one Friday night just over a week ago . . .

Harold Wangler shivered as he walked out of C.J.'s and down the deserted sidewalk to his car. The Florida air was slightly clammy on this late Friday night. It was dark. And it got suddenly darker when the lights shining from the hamburger joint went out. The manager of the Sea Palm Hotel had highly recommended C.J.'s for a burger and fries, but Harold wasn't sure the meal had been worth the hassle of dealing with the scatterbrained boy who had served him. Wangler had asked the kid to hold the pickle. So the boy had dutifully held the pickle—right under Harold's nose for several nauseating seconds. He had almost gotten sick to his stomach right on the table.

"Hold it right there, mister," a deep voice ordered.

Harold froze as something blunt and hard jabbed him in the back.

"Don't turn around. Just turn right and keep walking."

Nodding, Harold stepped toward the right and stumbled into the dark parking area beside the restaurant. The burger and fries churned in his stomach when the robber told him to stop and face the wall.

"Your wallet and your watch."

The voice sounded strange, Harold realized as he pulled out his wallet and ripped the watch off his wrist. The thief was disguising his voice to make it sound deeper than normal. Harold made a mental note so he wouldn't forget to tell the police. If he lived to tell the police . . .

"Turn around and you're dead," the voice said.

Harold fainted, collapsing in a heap on the pavement.

My best friends, Cindi Ornette and Noah Allen, hang out with me at C.J.'s all the time, but we stayed later that night, hoping to spot something or someone suspicious. There had been robberies near C.J.'s the past two Fridays, and the night manager, Jason Hopkins, was worried that the attacks would hurt business. Noah left first because he had to open the photo shop in the morning, but Cindi and I stuck it out until closing. After the night manager left for the bank and our friend Will Potter was ready to lock up, we headed back to Cindi's car together. The thief had only robbed people who were alone and we weren't taking any chances.

"I can't find my keys." Cindi patted her pockets, then rummaged through her bag.

"You had them in your hand right before we left the table." Shelby glanced over her shoulder just as Will turned off the lights in the restaurant. It was a moonless night and very dark.

"I thought I put them in my pocket. They must have fallen out." Cindi sighed. "We'll never find them in the dark. My flashlight's locked in the car."

"Shelby Woo to the rescue." Pulling a small flashlight out of her shoulder bag, Shelby flicked it on. "It's not very bright, but it's better than nothing."

Shaking her head, Cindi grinned. "You're the only girl I know who carries a flashlight in her purse."

"I'm a detective. It's standard equipment." Leading the way, Shelby scanned the ground as they retraced their steps back to C.J.'s. The keys were lying on the sidewalk in front of the darkened building.

"I can't believe we found them!" As Cindi stooped to pick up the lost keys, a police patrol car cruising down the empty street stopped in front of them.

A female officer rolled down the passenger window and leaned over. "It's a little late to be hanging out, isn't it, girls?"

Shelby aimed her flashlight at the officer's face, forcing the woman to shield her eyes. "Oh, hi, Officer Mendoza!"

"Shelby?" The woman frowned. "What are you doing here?"

"Looking for Cindi's car keys," Shelby answered honestly. Everyone at the station knew she had a knack for getting involved in police business. And everyone knew Detective Hineline strongly disapproved. "They must have fallen out of her pocket when we left C.J.'s."

"Right." The officer's eyes narrowed. "What are you doing at C.J.'s?"

"We hang out here all the time—"

Shelby's words were lost in the sound of a choked scream followed by a frantic, frightened voice. "Hey! What's going on?" Shelby shouted.

Officer Mendoza was out of her car in a flash, nightstick raised and ready. "You two stay here!"

As the woman dashed toward the side parking lot, Shelby and Cindi looked at each other.

"The robber?" Cindi asked, eyes wide with anticipation.

"Has to be." Without wasting another second, Shelby dashed after Tracy Mendoza with Cindi on her heels. They rounded the corner of the building just as the officer skidded to a halt several paces from two men. One man was crumpled on the ground. The other was leaning over him.

"Freeze, mister!" Mendoza barked.

It was impossible to see clearly in the dark. Anxious to be of assistance, Shelby beamed her flashlight on the standing man's face as he raised his head.

Shelby and Cindi both gasped in shocked surprise.

It was Will!

Chapter
2

"It's Saturday morning." Detective Hineline paused by Shelby's desk and eyed her suspiciously. "You're here kind of early, aren't you?"

"Yes, but that's because—"

"Later, Shelby." Spotting Tracy Mendoza walking through the door with Will, Hineline waved to the officer, directing her to join him in the interrogation room. Mendoza followed him inside, then closed the door.

Will hesitated uncertainly.

Catching his eye, Shelby stood up and motioned him over. Will had found Mr. Wangler lying on the driveway when he'd been dumping the restaurant's trash on his way home from work the night before. Officer Mendoza had asked him to stop by the station because he was a witness.

"Hey, Shelby!" Will looked around the bustling station with awed curiosity as he ambled toward her desk. "So this is where you work. Way cool!"

"Yeah." Shelby beamed as she moved to the front of her desk. "It certainly is."

"I've never been a witness to a crime before." Will's smile changed into a nervous frown. "What am I in for?"

"Don't worry," Shelby said gently. "They'll just ask you some questions." Will wasn't a complete moron like some people thought. His perspective was just slightly askew of everyone else's. "Besides, your parents are going to meet you here, aren't they?"

Will shook his head. "No. They're visiting my uncle in Miami this weekend. I couldn't go 'cause I had to work."

"Oh." Shelby frowned. It was normal policy to have parents present when kids under eighteen were interrogated. However, Will was at the station as a witness, not a suspect, so it was probably all right. "Well, that's okay. Just tell Detective Hineline what you saw. And relax."

"Cool." Stuffing his hands in his pockets, Will turned to look at the wanted posters on the wall. "I'm looking for Detective Hineline."

Shelby looked up as a middle-aged man wearing a flower-print shirt, Bermuda shorts, sandals, a straw hat and sunglasses entered and stopped a uniformed officer walking by. The third tourist robbery victim, Harold Wangler, was right on time.

"Officer Mendoza asked me to come in and fill out a robbery report for Detective Hineline."

Pointing the man toward Hineline's desk, the officer went into the interrogation room to get the detective.

Sinking into a chair to wait, Mr. Wangler looked at Shelby narrowly, then nodded in recognition. "You were there last night, weren't you?"

"Yes, I was." Shelby smiled brightly. "Did everything go okay at the hospital?"

"I'm fine. Just a bruise on my elbow from the fall and a severe case of indigestion. Probably from that greasy hamburger I ate." Mr. Wangler scowled as Will turned back around to look at the posters. "Or the stench of dill pickle."

"Well, I'm glad you're okay," Shelby said sincerely.

"I'm not okay at all! Getting robbed was the most terrifying thing that ever happened to me!" Mr. Wangler shuddered. "The sound of that voice will haunt me for a long time. It was disguised, you know? Like . . ." He paused thoughtfully.

"Like what?" Shelby prodded, leaning forward expectantly. Unnerved by the experience, the victim was anxious to talk. And Shelby, who was becoming more drawn into the case as it grew more complex, was eager to listen.

"The voice was like a woman trying to sound like a man, or a kid trying to sound older," Mr. Wangler explained.

"Oh, yeah. I know *exactly* what you mean," Will agreed enthusiastically. "Like this, right?" He lowered his voice to demonstrate. "Your wallet and your watch."

Shelby flinched. Will sounded like a bullfrog with a sore throat. *And apparently,* she thought grimly, *so did the thief.*

Detective Hineline and Officer Mendoza came out of the interrogation room and headed toward them.

"Yeah. *Just* like that!" Mr. Wangler's brown eyes narrowed behind his horn-rimmed glasses as he studied Will. "And come to think of it, the guy reeked of french fries—just like you!"

"What's going on here?" Detective Hineline asked sharply.

Shelby's heart fluttered. She had inadvertently thrown two witnesses together—three if she counted herself—by discussing the crime. If the credibility of Mr. Wangler's and Will's testimonies had been compromised as a result, it would be all her fault! But that wasn't the worst of it, Shelby realized with a sinking stomach. Mr. Wangler's next statement gave her a bigger reason to worry.

"It's him!" Mr. Wangler shook his finger at Will.

"Right!" Shelby interjected. "He's the one who found you after you were robbed."

Hineline fixed her with an annoyed frown. "Don't you have something to do?"

"No, no!" Mr. Wangler shouted. "That boy sounds exactly like—"

"Not here, Mr. Wangler!" Hineline silenced the man with a stern look, then turned to Officer Mendoza. "Take Mr. Wangler into the interrogation room and get him a cup of coffee. I'll be right there."

"Yes, sir." Giving Mr. Wangler a reassuring smile, Mendoza took his arm and steered him across the room.

Hineline glanced at his clipboard, then at Will with a questioning frown. "Are you Will Potter?"

"Yep." Will nodded and swallowed hard, nervous in spite of Shelby's assurances. His anxiety gave the impression that he was guilty of something.

"I think you'd better come with me, son."

"Where?" Will's eyes widened.

"To the other interrogation room," Hineline said.

Hineline's expression and tone hardened and the implication of *that* did not elude Shelby. Her head reeled as the meaning of the unexpected and sudden turn of events began to sink in. Will was totally oblivious of the change in his status, which suddenly shifted from witness to possible suspect.

"*Everyone* who hangs out at C.J.'s smells like french fries!" Shelby called out as Hineline led Will away. The detective ignored her.

Realizing she was responsible for Will's predicament because she had urged Mr. Wangler to talk, Shelby dashed back to her chair. She had to look busy when the detective returned so he wouldn't suspect she was up to anything. The idea that the easygoing, slightly befuddled Will had suddenly embarked on a life of crime was ludicrous. However, Hineline wouldn't consider anything but the facts in his investigation. If she was going to help Will, she had to have all the facts, too, including the details of Mr. Wangler's eyewitness account.

Watching from the corner of her eye, Shelby quickly turned back to her computer. As she expected, Hineline glanced toward her desk before he went into the interrogation room and closed the door. He had also stationed a uniformed officer to guard the room where Will was waiting.

Grabbing a stack of files, Shelby left her desk. No one noticed when she ducked into the narrow room with the speakers and surveillance mirror-window next to the interrogation room. Hugging the folders, Shelby tried to still her frantic pulse as she stared through the one-way glass. She could see and hear Hineline, Mendoza and Wangler, but they couldn't see or hear her— she hoped. She didn't know what the penalty was for listening in without authorization, but she was sure she wouldn't like it.

"Okay, Mr. Wangler," Hineline began as he took a seat at the long table. "Just tell us everything you remember."

Mr. Wangler cleared his throat. "I was hungry and the manager at my hotel suggested this C.J.'s place. He said they made real hamburgers—"

"What happened when you *left* C.J.'s?" Hineline asked, trying not to let his impatience show.

Shelby listened intently as Mr. Wangler recounted the crime. His memory was impressive. All too often, helpful details were forgotten because of the victim's fear. He could not, however, identify the blunt weapon the robber jammed into his back. It could have been something completely harmless, Shelby realized. *Even a finger.* Mr. Wangler had been too frightened to turn around and look.

"But I'm *sure* that boy I just saw is the robber," Mr. Wangler insisted. "He sounds just like the guy, and he saw how much money I had when I paid. He was *very* interested."

Nodding, Detective Hineline made a notation on his clipboard. "That's significant, Mr. Wangler, but it's not enough for us to act on."

Shelby almost sighed with relief, but the witness wasn't finished yet.

"There's more." Mr. Wangler sat back with a smug expression. "I heard him ask that pretty waitress out to dinner at Beach Avenue—the most exclusive and expensive restaurant in Cocoa Beach. What would that cost, huh? Fifty bucks a person, easy."

Startled, Shelby blinked. Linda Alvarez, the part-time waitress Jason had hired to help out on busy weekend nights, was beautiful and twenty-one. Sixteen and socially inept even by high school standards, Will didn't stand a chance.

Again, Hineline nodded, made a note, then looked at Officer Mendoza. "What do we know about the waitress?"

"Not much. Her name's Linda Alvarez and she started working at C.J.'s two weeks ago—according to Will." Mendoza rolled her eyes. "She's all he talked about on the way in this morning."

Mr. Wangler brightened. "A-hah! Two weeks! Didn't these robberies start two weeks ago?"

"This is *my* investigation, Mr. Wangler!" Hineline huffed. "You're the victim. I'm the detective."

"Well, Mr. Detective, that kid's got my money and I want it back!" The angry man hit the table with his fist.

Shelby glared at the blustering tourist through the glass. Mr. Wangler's bravado in the safety of the police station was maddening. If he hadn't fainted from fright the night before, he'd *know* Will couldn't possibly be guilty.

Hineline looked up suddenly and said dismissively, "That'll be all for now, Mr. Wangler." Standing up, he deftly escorted the surprised man out of the room. "We'll keep you informed. Have a nice day."

Bewildered, Shelby nibbled her lip. Detective Hineline had figured something out that he didn't want the victim to hear. Even though she was pressing her luck by staying to eavesdrop, she couldn't resist when the detective leveled Mendoza with a stern scowl.

"What?" Mendoza asked, curious.

"If Will Potter was the thief, he would have had Mr. Wangler's wallet in his possession last night."

Mendoza gasped.

Though she didn't know what Hineline was driving at, Shelby tensed.

"I was afraid of that." Hineline sagged with a weary sigh. "You didn't search Will at the scene, did you?"

"Uh—" Tracy Mendoza shook her head. "No, sir. I didn't. Will's story made sense, and it never crossed my mind that he might be the perp."

"That judgment call sure complicates things, doesn't it, Mendoza?" The woman nodded, and Hineline exhaled in frustration before saying, "We don't have the evidence to clear Will."

Shelby lowered her gaze. She had been on the scene last night, too, and was just as guilty of negligence as Officer Mendoza. Neither of them had even considered that Will might be the robber. A search would have *proven* he wasn't, if Mr. Wangler's wallet and watch weren't found in his pockets. Now, it was too late.

"We don't have evidence to arrest him, either." Detective Hineline stood up to leave. "Unless I can get him to confess."

Holding her breath, Shelby waited several seconds after Hineline and Mendoza left the room. Cracking the door, she peeked into the room, then slipped out when no one was looking.

Visibly frustrated because of her oversight at the crime scene, Tracy Mendoza trudged out of the station.

Hineline waved the guard away as he entered the other interrogation room to confront Will. The door did not completely close behind him.

Clutching the files, Shelby walked across the room. When she reached the door, which was still ajar, she paused. Flipping through the folders as though she were looking for one in particular, she listened.

"Just a couple of questions, Will. Then you can go," the detective said.

"Okay. I'm working the early shift at C.J.'s today and I don't want to be late."

"This will just take a minute," Hineline said. "Did you see Mr. Wangler open his wallet when he paid his bill?"

"I'll say." Will whistled. "I don't see too many hundred-dollar bills at C.J.'s, and that guy had a whole bunch of them."

Shelby winced and glanced helplessly at the door. Honest and naive, Will was incriminating himself without even realizing it.

"I understand you asked Ms. Alvarez out to dinner."

"Yeah, but she turned me down . . . again."

"How did you expect to pay for dinner at Beach Avenue if she had accepted?" Hineline asked sympathetically.

Shelby pushed the door open. "Excuse me."

Hineline's eyes flashed. "This better be good."

"Won't Will's rights and the case be compromised if he doesn't have a legal advisor?"

"If he was under arrest, yes," Hineline said. "But he's not. He's here of his own free will."

"I don't need a lawyer, Shelby." Sighing heavily, Will looked at the detective, then stared into space with an expression of lovesick longing as he answered the question. "I've been saving up ever since Linda started working at C.J.'s."

"Thank you, Will. You can go now." Hineline

stood aside to let him pass. "But don't leave town."

"Okay." Nodding, Will darted out the door. "See ya later, Shelby."

Waving absently, Shelby stopped Hineline as he moved past her. "For the record, I was at C.J.'s last night."

"Yeah, so?" Hineline hesitated impatiently.

"So—everyone there saw Mr. Wangler flash a wad of hundred-dollar bills." Noting Hineline's curious frown, Shelby qualified the remark to cover the fact that she'd been eavesdropping. "I thought it might be important. That so *many* people knew he was carrying all that money."

"I'll keep that in mind. Finish your filing."

Shelby's spirits took a dive as Hineline walked back to his desk. Even though Mr. Wangler's reasoning was flimsy, Will *was* on the scene, he *did* smell like french fries, and he *also* sounded like the thief when he lowered his voice. She didn't believe for one second that he was guilty, but that wasn't enough. She had to *prove* he was innocent.

Because if the real tourist robber wasn't found, the shadow of suspicion would always hang over Will.

Chapter
3

"Will? A suspect?" Cindi laughed as she flicked a feather duster over the display shelves in the photo shop. She stopped abruptly when she saw Shelby's serious expression. "No way!"

"That is totally ridiculous." Noah inserted the last photo-packet into the alphabetized file under the counter. "Will isn't conniving enough to be a crook."

"Tell that to Detective Hineline." Shelby sagged against the counter and sighed. Business was slow for a Saturday afternoon, so her friends had time to talk. "I don't really blame him, though. He's under a lot of pressure from the city to catch the robber before the bad press kills the tourist trade. And Will's the only suspect he's got."

A customer rushed into the store. Shelby waited quietly while Noah searched the file for the woman's order and Cindi finished dusting a row of cameras.

"The thing is," Cindi said when the customer had gone, "the robber could be anyone in Cocoa Beach."

"Maybe, but I don't think so. There's a connection to C.J.'s." Shelby began to pace in front of the counter. "The robberies all happened outside C.J.'s on Friday nights. And I'm sure the thief was *inside* the restaurant not too long before closing."

"What makes you think so?" Noah asked.

"Mr. Wangler was very definite about smelling french fries. That's one of the reasons Detective Hineline thinks Will might be guilty. But anyone who hangs out there long enough leaves smelling like fries."

Cindi grimaced. "Don't I know it! My mom has given up trying to wash the odor out of my clothes."

"That still doesn't narrow things down much," Noah said. "C.J.'s is really busy on Friday nights. Lots of people were there."

"But *lots* of people didn't see Mr. Wangler's wallet full of hundred-dollar bills," Shelby pointed out. "Only a few people did."

"Like you and me." Cindi frowned thoughtfully. "And what about the night manager, Jason, and that new waitress—what's her name?"

"Linda Alvarez." Shelby smiled. "Would you believe Will has a major crush on her?"

Noah rolled his eyes. "Talk about setting yourself up for a fall. Will's got a better chance of making genius scores on an IQ test than he does of going out with her."

"Sad, but it's all beside the point," Shelby said. "Linda began working at C.J.'s the same night the robberies started. That might not be a coincidence."

"It is kind of suspicious, huh?" Cindi brightened at the prospect of a solid suspect other than Will.

"In fact," Shelby added, "the robber was probably in C.J.'s all three Friday nights. Linda definitely was."

"You think a woman could have robbed three grown men?" Noah asked skeptically.

Cindi fixed him with an annoyed look. "Why not? The thief scared them into cooperating by jamming something into their backs."

Noah shrugged. "Sorry."

Shelby was too intent on isolating additional suspects to worry about Noah's remark. "Linda's younger brother stopped by, too." Her eyes narrowed as she thought back.

Peter Alvarez came in to return his sister's car. . . .

"Thanks for letting me use the car, Linda. It's parked across the street." Peter stood by the counter with a backpack slung over one shoulder. He held out the keys.

"Just a minute, Peter." Arms loaded with burger baskets, Linda dashed past him on her way to the outside patio tables.

"Hurry, okay?" Peter called after her. "It's a long walk home." Sinking onto a stool, Peter impatiently drummed his fingers on the counter and glanced around the almost empty restaurant.

Shelby didn't recognize the boy. Either he went to a different school or he was new in town.

Scooping up a basket of fries and a burger, Will rushed over to Mr. Wangler's table. The man's eyes widened as he set the food down.

"I told you to hold the pickle!"

"Oh, yeah! Right!" Grinning, Will picked up

the pickle spear and held it in front of Mr. Wangler's face.

Mr. Wangler gagged and shoved Will's hand aside, sending the pickle spear sailing across the room. "Give me my bill. Now! Then go away and stay away!"

"Sure." Totally unperturbed, Will shrugged and returned to the counter.

Tossing the keys to Linda, Peter slipped the backpack over both shoulders. On his way out, he looked at Mr. Wangler as Will waited for the man to pay his bill.

Peter saw Mr. Wangler open his wallet and thumb through all those hundred-dollar bills. . . .

"But he didn't stay long and he left half an hour before closing." Shelby rubbed her chin. "We have to find out if Peter was at C.J.'s the other two Friday nights. I'll check with Will."

"We know Jason was there all three Fridays," Noah said.

"But he left for the bank ten minutes before midnight." Cindi absently dusted the counter. "Mr. Wangler was robbed at twelve-ten. Twenty minutes later."

"But Jason could have robbed Mr. Wangler *be-*

fore he went to the bank." Shelby resumed pacing. "Unfortunately, there's no way to check the exact time he put the bag in the night deposit drop."

Shelby really didn't want Jason to be guilty, either. An aspiring artist who worked part-time in construction and managed C.J.'s on weekend nights to pay his bills, he was always pleasant and treated his teenaged customers with respect. *He's also totally cute,* she thought, *but I can't let any of that influence my investigation.* Jason was a suspect whether she liked it or not.

So was Cory Conrad.

Cory sat at that corner table for two hours before closing, acting like a complete jerk, as usual.

"Do you want another soda, Cory?" Will asked for about the tenth time.

"Get lost!" Cory's blue eyes flashed with angry warning.

"I do that sometimes," Will said agreeably. *"Not in here, though. C.J.'s isn't big enough to get lost in. So what about that soda?"*

"No!" Cory's empty glass rattled as he

slammed his fist into the table. He turned his attention back to Jason as Will ambled away.

"Cory Conrad is such a creep." Cindi exhaled with disgust, then nibbled on a french fry.

"He's awfully interested in Jason for some reason." Shelby shifted her attention between the two as she nursed her third lemonade. Jason was handling take-out orders and answering the phone. Ordinarily, the night manager wouldn't let someone occupy a table for so long without ordering anything. Either Jason was too busy to notice Cory's riveted stare or he was deliberately avoiding it. Curious, Shelby watched and wondered.

Cory didn't take his eyes off Jason for more than a few seconds—except when Mr. Wangler shuffled through his wallet.

"Cory Conrad! Yuck." Cindi shuddered, turning away from the shelf of cameras. "He thinks he's so tough."

"He is," Noah said. "He's the biggest bully in school, and he's got the left-hook to back it up."

"*Was* the biggest bully," Shelby corrected. "He graduated."

"Lucky for us." Noah scowled. "Maybe he'll

27

leave town this fall to terrorize an unsuspecting college campus."

"No doubt," Cindi huffed. "What's Cory got against the world and everyone in it, anyway? He's got looks and his father's rich."

"That's right." Noah glanced at Shelby. "So why would he rob people and risk going to jail?"

"Why would any of our suspects?" Shelby countered. "Maybe Cory's dad doesn't give him much money. Money may not even *be* the motive."

"Yeah, but . . ." Cindi looked at Shelby expectantly. "Maybe one of our suspects needs extra cash really bad—enough to risk getting caught."

"Nailing down a motive will do for starters," Shelby agreed, sensing Cindi's eagerness to dive into the case. "If none of the suspects can prove what time they got home last night, we might not be able to eliminate anyone on the basis of opportunity."

"Noah and I get off soon," Cindi quickly volunteered. "We can talk with Linda's neighbors. Maybe someone saw her drive in. Peter, too. We'll check it out."

"Posing as what?" Noah asked, leaning on the counter. "The curfew cops?"

"You're the actor, Noah." Cindi smiled impishly. "You'll think of something."

"And while you're at it," Shelby added, "clock how long it takes to walk from here to there. I'll see what I can find out from Jason."

"What about Cory?" Cindi asked.

"*I'm* not tackling Cory," Noah said stubbornly. "I like my nose just the way it is."

"I'll worry about Cory later. We don't even know if he was at C.J.'s when all three victims were robbed." Shelby understood Noah's reluctance. He didn't want to set himself up as a target for Cory's hair-trigger temper. Or his notorious left-hook.

Neither do I, Shelby thought uneasily. *But I'm a detective, and courting danger goes with the territory.*

Chapter
4

"I can't believe none of Linda's neighbors are home." Cindi paused on the sidewalk, tapping her foot in frustration. Everyone was probably out doing Saturday afternoon errands.

The houses in the modest residential area were small, and only a few of the yards were landscaped. Patches of sand spotted most of the lawns, but several coconut palms lined the narrow street. Cindi noticed that the dead fronds dangling below their green crowns needed trimming. It was definitely a neighborhood in need of attention.

"At least now we know it takes twenty minutes to walk here from C.J.'s," Noah pointed out.

"So Peter should have gotten home before midnight."

"If he came straight home," Noah emphasized.

"Right. Guess we'll have to try a slightly different version of Plan A."

Noah glanced at Cindi warily. "Like what?"

"Like trying to sell magazines to Linda Alvarez."

To Cindi's surprise, Noah didn't argue like he usually did when she wanted to confront a suspect head-on. Pencil and pad in hand, he followed her up the walk to the front door. Donning a charming smile, she rang the doorbell.

Peter opened the door. "Yes?"

"Hi!" Cindi said brightly.

"Hi." Peter nodded with a questioning look at Cindi. "Do I know you?"

"I don't think so . . ." Cindi hesitated. She had been sitting with her back to Peter the night before at C.J.'s. He couldn't possibly recognize her—could he?

Noah pressed forward. "We're selling magazines to send some worthy, underprivileged kids to Space Camp."

"Is your si—mother home?" Cindi coughed to cover her near blunder. Fortunately, Peter didn't seem to notice.

"I live with my older sister. Our, uh . . . parents were killed in a car crash last year."

"Oh, my. I'm sorry. I . . . uh . . ." Cindi faltered.

Peter shrugged, then smiled to put them at ease. "Linda's out grocery shopping, but if you want to come in and leave the information—"

"Sure." Noah quickly accepted the invitation. "One kid goes to camp for—"

"—every ten subscriptions we get." Cindi stepped inside behind Noah and jumped as the screen door banged closed. They both stared when Peter held out his hand.

"The subscription information?" he prompted.

"Oh. Uh . . ." Cindi cleared her throat. They didn't have any magazine information. "Right. I, uh . . ."

Noah slapped his forehead. "I forgot. We gave the last pamphlet to some guy down the street. Anything that involves space is a *really* big deal in this town. But if you want, we can stop back—"

"Never mind. We can't afford any magazines right now anyway." Peter sighed. "To be honest, I asked you in because I've been kinda starved for company. We just moved in three weeks ago, and since school's out for the summer, I haven't met anybody, yet."

"Where are you from?" Relieved, Cindi quickly recovered her composure.

"Atlanta. Linda heard the job opportunities down here were pretty good. So here we are. I'm Peter Alvarez."

"Glad to meet you. I'm Cindi Ornette and he's Noah Allen."

"Did you win all those?" Noah whistled as he walked over to a bookcase filled with track-and-field trophies and framed ribbons.

"Yeah." Peter grinned with shy pride. "Hopefully, I'll make the team at Space Coast High, too. I won't be going to college unless I get an athletic scholarship."

"Hasn't your sister found a good job yet?" Cindi asked.

Peter rolled his eyes. "Two of them. She's got an okay job as a receptionist during the day, but I sure wish she didn't have to wait tables on weekends."

"That's tough." Cindi nodded sympathetically.

"Yeah, but we gotta eat and pay the rent. She won't let me go to work because she wants me to concentrate on school and track. I do some

3 3

odd jobs here and there, but it's not enough. And that C.J.'s place is the pits."

"C.J.'s!" Cindi pretended to look appalled. "No wonder you're upset!"

"Upset?" Peter paused uncertainly.

Noah pounced on the opening. "I would be if my sister worked at the scene of all those robberies."

"Oh, yeah." Peter nodded. "You've got that right. I worry myself sick waiting for her to get home."

"I'll bet," Cindi said. "She probably gets off really late, too."

"Midnight, but it's only a five-minute drive."

"That late, huh?" Taking a deep breath, Noah glanced significantly at Cindi. "So . . ."

"So . . ." Cindi hesitated, grasping for some way to prompt Peter into revealing the time of Linda's arrival without seeming *too* obvious. "You were probably a nervous wreck last night until she got home at . . ."

"Twelve-ten or so." Peter sighed despondently. "Bone-tired and cranky after waiting on all those hungry people. The guy she works with is a nice kid, but not too bright."

"To put it mildly," Noah quipped.

Cindi nudged him, then smiled at Peter. "All the kids hang out there."

"Yeah?" Peter looked up with sudden interest. "Maybe I should hang out at C.J.'s on Friday nights, too. You know, to meet more kids. Instead of going to the movies by myself."

"Do you go to the movies every Friday?" Cindi blurted out.

"Beats staying home alone. Last night I saw a double feature at the Vintage Drive-In. Florida may be the only state left that still has operating drive-in movies."

"California probably does, too," Noah said.

"Gotta go, Peter." Tugging on Noah's sleeve, Cindi urged him toward the door. "See ya around."

"Sure." Peter blinked as they rushed outside.

"What's the hurry, Cindi?" Noah asked when they reached the sidewalk. "He was just getting warmed up."

"He spends Fridays at the movies—not at C.J.'s."

"He was at C.J.'s last night," Noah reminded her.

"For ten minutes tops. To return his sister's car, which he borrowed to go to the drive-in. And unless Linda's figured out how to be in two places at once, she couldn't be the thief. She got home at twelve-ten."

"So Peter says." Noah raised an eyebrow.

"Why would he lie?" Cindi frowned, then looked up sharply. "To protect his sister?"

"Who just happens to be his sole source of financial support?" Noah shrugged. "Could be."

"Let's check out the neighbors again." Cindi strode down the sidewalk with renewed determination. Everybody had at least *one* nosey neighbor. Unless Linda Alvarez was the rare exception, someone on the street must have noticed what time she had gotten home.

It had taken Shelby an hour to think of a convincing reason for stopping by to see Jason. Usually, she would just pretend to be someone else in order to question suspects or witnesses in a case. Acting gigs were one of the perks of her chosen profession. This time, assuming a glamorous identity just wasn't possible.

Although Cindi went to C.J.'s as often as Shelby, she might have been able to avoid being recognized by the weekend night manager with a clever disguise. Cindi was just one of a hundred nameless kids who frequented the burger joint, and she had never spoken to Jason Hopkins directly. Shelby, on the other hand, had picked up too many take-out orders for guests at her grandfather's bed-and-breakfast, the Easterly Breeze. But she never missed an opportunity to talk to the handsome, struggling young artist. She didn't even have to fake being interested in his artistic career. And *that* had not escaped Jason's attention. Nothing short of drastic plastic surgery could prevent him from recognizing her.

She had finally decided that Jason's art was the only sure way to approach him without making him suspicious. And her cover story wouldn't be a total lie. Maybe someday her grandfather really would decide to redecorate the bed-and-breakfast using paintings by local artists. Even so, Shelby felt a twinge of guilt about the deception. The only thing Jason cared about was his art work.

Besides, Shelby thought, *if his answers to my questions prove he couldn't possibly be the tourist robber, I'll be doing him a huge favor.* She tried not to think about the alternative as she cut across the vacant lot behind Jason's two-room bungalow. Her faith in human nature and her own instincts would be severely shaken if he turned out to be guilty.

All thoughts about Jason were temporarily

shoved aside as Shelby started around the end of his front porch.

Cory Conrad was stomping up the steps toward Jason's front door.

And he looked fighting mad.

Shelby ducked.

"What a cute little dog!" Cindi gushed over the curly haired canine that was yapping hysterically and straining at its leash.

"Yeah, he's a real macho mutt, all right." Noah smiled tightly, but kept his distance from the elderly man walking the snarling dog. The man lived directly across the street from Peter and Linda Alvarez.

"Quiet, Caesar! Sit!"

The little dog growled indignantly and sat down.

Cindi quickly engaged the man in conversation. "You know, it's really a fortunate coincidence that we ran into you, Mr.—"

"MacDougal." The man frowned suspiciously. "Why?"

"Because . . ." Cindi fumbled for a reason.

"We're doing a survey on . . ." Noah was at a loss.

"The, uh . . . nocturnal habits of local dogs," Cindi finished.

"Why?" Mr. MacDougal asked again.

"Noise." Noah said the first thing that came into his mind, but it was perfect. Sighing to emphasize the seriousness of the matter, he adopted the stern, self-important attitude of a city official. "Cocoa Beach has a strict noise ordinance. Does your dog bark at night?"

"No."

"Not even when he has to go outside to . . . you know?" Cindi asked.

"I take Caesar out *every* night at *exactly* twelve-fifteen. He doesn't have to bark."

"I see." Noah frowned thoughtfully. The man was getting nervous and seemed anxious to defend his dog. "He's barking at us now," Noah pointed out. "Doesn't he bark at the neighbors? If they come home late or something?"

"No. That new woman across the street drove in while we were outside last night and Caesar didn't make a peep!"

"After twelve-fifteen?" Cindi asked excitedly.

"More like twelve-twenty-five, I'd say. About five minutes after her brother finished running. Caesar didn't bark at *him*, either."

"Her brother goes running after midnight?" Noah asked.

Mr. MacDougal rolled his eyes. "That kid runs all the time. He must go around this block a hundred times a day. And he always carries a wooden stick, like he's training for some race or something."

"Thanks for your time and cooperation, Mr. MacDougal," Noah said.

"And don't worry about Caesar being in any trouble," Cindi added. "It's the three A.M. barkers the city is trying to control."

When Caesar jumped up and started barking again, Noah pulled Cindi away. He couldn't wait to report back to Shelby. It had taken Linda Alvarez twenty-five minutes to make a five-minute drive home! She had had more than enough time to rob Mr. Wangler.

Moving as quietly as possible, Shelby climbed Jason's porch steps after Jason let Cory into the house. The front window was open in spite of the summer heat and humidity. *A point in Jason's favor*, Shelby thought. If he had stolen Mr. Wangler's money, he could afford to run the air conditioner. Then she realized he didn't have an air conditioner.

Pressing against the house, Shelby chanced a peek inside. Wearing a paint-splattered T-shirt and cutoffs, Jason stood with folded arms while Cory paced. The artist wore his long, dark hair tied back at the neck at C.J.'s because of Health Department regulations. Now, it hung loose to his shoulders. Jason nervously brushed it behind his ears as Cory started to yell.

"Nobody else would loan you money for art show fees and supplies, Hopkins! A wanna-be artist is not exactly a sound investment."

"I know. If it wasn't for you, I wouldn't have been able to enter the Cocoa Beach Sidewalk Art Show next weekend. I really appreciate it." Jason sighed.

"I don't want your appreciation," Cory sneered. "I want my thousand bucks."

Jason nodded patiently. "And you'll get it. Next Saturday afternoon at three. Just like we agreed."

"It'll be twelve hundred next Saturday."

Shelby's eyes widened. Cory was a loan shark who lent money to desperate people, then charged outrageous interest fees! *Worse*, she thought with a sinking heart. Jason owed him a bundle. Shelby had managed to sneak a peek at Hineline's case file. The money stolen from Mr.

Wangler and the other two victims totaled just over seven hundred dollars. That wasn't enough to cover Jason's debt to Cory, but Jason still had a week to come up with the rest.

If he's the thief, Shelby reminded herself. She desperately didn't want the handsome artist to be guilty.

"And you'd better have all of it or else!" Cory shook his fist in Jason's face.

"Or else what?" Jason wasn't impressed.

"Or else—" Cory glanced around the room, then walked over to a carpenter's apron lying on the floor.

Jason probably wears that when he's working on a construction job, Shelby thought as Cory leaned over and pulled something out of a pocket in the apron.

"Or else I'm going to punch holes in your precious paintings," Cory answered.

Shelby stifled a gasp as Cory lunged at the nearest canvas with a huge nail. Jason jumped to stop him, but Cory stopped himself—just short of shoving the four-inch spike through a picture of a two-masted ketch under full-sail on a rolling blue sea.

"You wouldn't dare!" Jason glared at the teenager, his face pale and drawn.

"It's your decision, Hopkins. Get me the money, or the paintings are trashed." Pocketing the nail, Cory turned abruptly and charged for the door.

Shelby jumped back, ready to dive over the porch railing to avoid getting caught eavesdropping. She wasn't prepared to face Cory Conrad any more than Jason was. Especially since Cory was obviously in a worse mood than usual.

Her shirttail snagged on a protruding nail holding the screen frame in place. Shelby yanked herself free just as Cory burst outside and whirled to face her. His icy blue eyes narrowed and his jaw flexed. Speaking through clenched teeth, his voice was a spine-chilling rasp of barely contained fury.

"Nobody spies on *me* and gets away with it!"

Uh-oh.

Chapter
5

"Hi, Cory." Shelby dropped to her hands and knees on the porch and began a frantic search. "I lost an earring here somewhere. Do you see it?"

"You're not wearing earrings, Shelby," Cory said flatly.

"I know. I lost it!" Standing up, Shelby huffed in irritation. She hoped she looked convincing. There was no telling what Cory might do if he knew she knew he was a loan shark. Loan-sharking was illegal.

"So where's the other one?" he scoffed.

Shelby sighed heavily. "I lost that one at the beach last month."

"What's going on out here?" Jason peered through the screen door.

"It better be nothing." Cory said. He cast a menacing glance at Shelby as he started down the steps. "Keep your nose out of my business, Shelby, or you'll be sorry. Really sorry."

Relieved, Shelby watched as Cory stormed down the sidewalk and got into a red sports car parked a short distance down the street. The car, a very expensive model, looked brand-new.

"If the chip on Cory's shoulder was any heavier, he'd be permanently lopsided," Jason said.

Shelby laughed as the young artist lowered one shoulder to demonstrate. Not only was Jason talented, gorgeous and incredibly nice, he had a sense of humor, too. Not even in her wildest imagination could she picture him robbing a tourist in a back alley.

Watch it! Shelby cautioned herself. A good detective didn't let her feelings interfere with an investigation.

"So what can I do for you, Shelby?"

"Me? Uh . . ." Shelby was so busy mentally cataloging information, she almost forgot why she was there. From listening to Jason and Cory's conversation, she had found out a lot—except what time Jason got home last night. "My grandfather and I had this idea, and you were the first artist I thought of. But you're probably tired after working so late . . ."

"Not really. I wanted to get an early start at the easel because I've got a remodeling job this afternoon. So I came right home and went to bed. What's your idea?"

"Oh. Well . . ." Shelby forced herself to sound enthusiastic. "We were thinking that if we displayed paintings by local artists on the walls at the bed-and-breakfast, some of our guests might buy them."

"That's a great gimmick." Jason smiled and nodded. "Count me in."

"Really? Thanks! I'll let you know, okay?" Grinning, Shelby waved and dashed down the steps. Her smile fled the minute Jason went back inside and pulled the shades. If she couldn't find a witness who knew what time he had gotten home, she couldn't cross him off the suspect list.

Huddled around the corner table at C.J.'s, Shelby and her friends compared notes. Shelby struggled to shake off a grim mood. Noah and Cindi's witness, Mr. MacDougal, had confirmed that Linda had time to commit the crime before arriving home. But Shelby had struck out on Jason's block. Posing as a summer student employee of an insurance agency, she had pretended to be taking a survey. During her interviews with Jason's neighbors, she had casually mentioned that his old wreck fit the description of a car the agency was trying to locate because it had been involved in an accident the night before. However, no one had noticed what time the artist arrived home.

"You had a run-in with Cory?" Cindi gasped as Shelby recounted her close call with the bully.

"Not on purpose, believe me! I don't know where he was at twelve-ten last night, but I did get some very interesting information." Shelby paused to glance around. Except for a young couple totally engrossed with each other at an umbrella table outside, and Will, who was vigorously cleaning the grill, they had the restaurant to themselves.

"What?" Noah asked impatiently.

Shelby leaned forward and whispered, "For one thing, Cory's a loan shark."

"That's against the law," Cindi whispered back.

"Right, but even if we could get him arrested for that, it wouldn't help prove Will *isn't* the robber."

"And," Noah said glumly, "if Cory's getting

47

super-high interest rates, he probably isn't hurting for cash."

"Not necessarily." Shelby nodded thoughtfully. "Where does he get the money he loans?"

Noah shrugged. "From his rich father?"

"Maybe, but he's also got a brand-new, very expensive sports car. I don't think he could possibly be making enough in interest to pay for it. Not if he's loaning money to kids and struggling artists like Jason."

Cindi's eyes widened. "Jason owes him money?"

Shelby sighed. "A *lot* of money. And if he doesn't pay it back on time, Cory threatened to ruin his paintings."

"So Jason's got a motive to steal."

"Yeah," Cindi agreed. "But so does Linda Alvarez. She's working two jobs just to make ends meet, and she can't afford to send Peter to college."

Noah looked up and nudged Cindi to be quiet.

Sitting with her back to the room and the door, Shelby didn't see Will come up behind her. She jumped as he reached past her to put a basket of fries on the table.

"Sorry it took so long," Will apologized.

Shelby stopped him as he turned to leave. She still had a question that needed answering.

"Does Cory Conrad come in here every Friday night?"

Will nodded. "Yep. At least for the past few weeks he has. The guy always sits at this table and orders a soda. Then he spends the whole night staring at Jason. Weird, huh?"

"Yeah, thanks." Shelby smiled. "Don't worry, okay? Just because the police think you're the tourist robber . . ." The rest of her words trailed off as Noah deliberately spilled the basket of fries on the floor and ducked under the table with Cindi. ". . . doesn't mean that we do," Shelby finished, looking perplexed.

"I'm not worried." Will peered under the table. "Do you want to eat them off the floor or should I clean them up?"

Noah and Cindi frantically waved him away.

Out of the corner of her eye, Shelby saw Linda and Peter Alvarez walking to the counter. That explained why Noah and Cindi had gone into instant hiding. They didn't want Peter to see them at the crime scene so soon after questioning him.

Resting her face on her hand, Shelby turned slightly to watch. She didn't want Peter or Linda to know she was overly interested in them, but she was worried that they had overheard what she said to Will. Since no charges had been filed, no one except the police, herself and her friends knew that Will was the primary suspect in the tourist robbery case. A rumor like that could be all over town within a few hours.

Except, Shelby realized with relief, *Peter doesn't know anyone in Cocoa Beach to tell. He goes to the movies on Fridays by himself. And he obviously isn't hanging out at the beach or the mall, where he's likely to meet any of our school friends soon.* Wearing a stained T-shirt, torn jeans and bulky gloves, Peter was dressed for construction work, not play.

Forgetting Shelby and the dumped fries, Will ran back to the counter. "Hi, Linda," he said. Shoving his hands in his pockets, he rocked back and forth with nervous excitement. "Guess we're working together again today, huh?"

"Yes, we are, Will." Rolling her eyes as she turned away, Linda went into the office to get an apron.

Shelby felt a pang of compassion for the love-sick boy. Linda Alvarez obviously wasn't inter-ested in Will, but it was easy to understand why he was so smitten with her. Even with her long, dark hair tied back, wearing jeans and a C.J.'s shirt, she was really pretty.

Shelby tensed as Peter stared intently at Will, then relaxed when he just asked to borrow a pen. Either Peter hadn't heard her reference to Will being a police suspect or he didn't care.

"Linda told Jason I was handy with a hammer, so he offered me a couple hours' work on a re-modeling job," Peter explained. "I want to write down the address before I forget it."

"Sure!" Always eager to please, Will gave him the C.J.'s pen tucked over his left ear. He had another one stashed over the right ear. Shelby smiled fondly. Will was always walking around with pens over his ears because he forgot they were there.

Peter scribbled on the back of a paper napkin, then shoved the napkin and the pen into his pocket when Linda returned with the car keys. "Thanks, Linda. I'll be back at nine to pick you up."

"Don't be late. And make sure the gas tank's not empty, okay?" Linda eyed him sternly.

"Okay!" Shaking his head, Peter ran for the door.

Shelby looked under the table at Noah and Cindi. "Coast is clear."

Groaning, Noah stood up and put the basket of fries back on the table. "I think these fries have outlived their usefulness. They are no longer fit to consume."

"But they served a higher purpose," Shelby said. "That was quick thinking, Noah. I'm impressed."

"And I'm starved." Cindi sat down and brushed dust off her shorts and bare knees. "Let's get another basket."

Will was taking a phone order, so Linda came to the table. She frowned when Noah asked for another basket of fries. "Is something wrong with those?"

"No. They, uh . . . fell on the floor." Noah shrugged.

"Oh." Linda glanced over her shoulder at Will. He blushed and waved.

"Will didn't drop them." Noah quickly corrected her unspoken assumption. "I did."

"Well, that's too bad. I'll have to charge you for the second order then." Slipping her pen and pad into her apron, Linda picked up the basket.

"Will doesn't drop stuff *that* often," Cindi said, rising to Will's defense.

Linda blinked. "Of course he doesn't. He's very . . . dedicated to his work. And everyone seems to like him."

"Yes, we do," Shelby said emphatically.

Linda smiled. "So do I. Will's a sweet kid. C.J.'s wouldn't be nearly as much fun without him."

"That's the truth, but how come you're working in this place?" Noah asked bluntly. "I mean, C.J.'s isn't exactly one of the in-spots of Cocoa Beach."

"Unless you're a teenager," Shelby added.

Linda shrugged. "This was the only weekend job I could get because it's the off-season. I'm hoping to find something better in the fall. To be honest, I'm not making nearly enough here, but it's better than nothing."

There was truth to that, Shelby realized. Even though people came to visit the Space Center in July and August, the number of summer tourists was small compared to the hoards that came to Florida in winter. Even so, most of the area restaurants remained open in the off-season. It was hard to believe a sharp, pretty woman like Linda couldn't find a better weekend job.

Unless, Shelby thought as the waitress walked away, *Linda just doesn't want to leave a place where it's so easy to rob unsuspecting tourists.*

Noah frowned. "You don't really think she did it, do you, Shelby?"

"I don't know what to think." Shelby sighed.

"We've got three suspects who need a lot of extra money. First there's Linda Alvarez. She's struggling to pay her bills and, according to Mr. MacDougal, she had time to do the crime. Then there's Jason Hopkins. We don't know what time he got home, but we do know he owes Cory Conrad hundreds of dollars. And finally, Cory Conrad. We don't know what time he got home, either, but he loans people large sums of money and drives a very expensive car." Troubled, Shelby frowned.

"What's the matter?" Cindi asked.

"All we have is circumstantial evidence that doesn't *prove* anything. We need hard evidence and there isn't any."

"There isn't?" Noah asked, confused.

Shelby shook her head. "No. None of the wallets, watches or credit cards have turned up anywhere. I heard Detective Hineline complaining about it this morning after Mr. Wangler and Will left."

"So why don't you tell him about the other suspects?" Cindi asked. "Then he could get search warrants to look for that stuff where they live."

"You've got to be kidding! If Detective Hineline knows I'm investigating, I'll be in all kinds of trouble." Shelby shuddered. "Besides, he can't get search warrants on a kid's say-so or because he's got a hunch."

"But there's got to be *something* we can do!"

"Oh, there is, Cindi." Shelby's eyes sparkled.

Noah looked at the ceiling, then closed his eyes. "I'm afraid to ask."

"I'm not!" Cindi leaned forward expectantly. "What?"

"Detective Hineline needs to prove probable cause to conduct a search." Shelby winked. "We don't."

Chapter
6

"This contraption itches, Shelby." Taking off his bulky glove, Noah eased his hand under the flap of the canvas helmet to scratch his nose. "This has got to be the hottest Tuesday we've had all summer, too."

Shelby suppressed a grin and tugged on the black netting that covered her own face. The protective beekeeper headgear was itchy, but the dense mesh totally disguised her and Noah. It hadn't taken her long to come up with a plan to get Noah and herself *into* the Alvarez house and Peter *out* without being recognized. However, it had taken a few days to convince a local beekeeper to loan her the cumbersome suits for a few hours. The pesticide canisters they carried were filled with plain water.

"What if Linda didn't go to work today?" Noah asked as they headed up the front walk. "Or Peter won't leave?"

"Don't worry," Shelby said confidently. Infatuated, Will had learned a lot about Linda's life during his shy conversations with her at C.J.'s, including where she worked during the week. Shelby had called Parsons' Products and pretended to have a wrong number when Linda answered the phone. No problem there. She was almost positive getting rid of Peter wouldn't be a problem, either.

Peter frowned when he opened the door. "Yes?"

"Health Department." Noah dropped his voice to a deeper tone. "Sorry to inconvenience you, sir, but you'll have to leave while we inspect the premises. Killer bees have been sighted in this neighborhood."

"Those deadly African bees?" Peter's eyes widened in alarm and he bolted out the door.

"We might be a while," Noah said. "If you have something else to do . . ."

"I guess it wouldn't hurt to put in another five miles today." Reaching inside the door, Peter grabbed a twelve-inch length of cylindrical wood from his backpack. Then he took off down the sidewalk at a brisk jog.

"*Another* five miles?" Noah shook his head. "That's one dedicated athlete."

"So he won't be gone long. Let's get moving." Shelby hurried inside. Although pleased with how easily the ploy had worked, she wasn't thrilled about tricking Peter into leaving so they could look for the wallets and watches. But she didn't have any choice. None of the stolen property had surfaced, and Will was still Hineline's only suspect.

Setting their gloves, headgear and canisters by the front door, Shelby and Noah scoured the interior of the Alvarez house. Being careful not to mess up anything, they went through drawers, looked under the beds, peeked into closets and checked the kitchen cabinets. After twenty minutes, Shelby was convinced that the evidence was not stashed in the house.

"Linda wouldn't want Peter to find out she was a thief." Shelby slipped on her helmet and gloves.

"*If* she's the thief." Adjusting his own gear, Noah handed a canister to Shelby as they stepped outside.

"But if she is, she might not chance hiding the evidence inside where her brother might find it." Pulling a phony Health Department certificate out of her pocket, Shelby stuck the paper in the door. Cindi had composed and printed it on her dad's computer, but it looked real. The notice declared that no killer bees had been found. She didn't want Peter calling the official agency to ask.

"Let's check the backyard." Without giving Noah a chance to protest, Shelby dashed to the back of the house.

Weeds had overgrown the wooden flower boxes on the ground around the cement patio. While she sifted through the crumbling Spanish moss lining the boxes, Noah inspected several hanging baskets. Unlike the boxes, the wire bowls were filled with blossoming plants. He prodded them with the long metal nozzle attached to the canister by a hose.

"Shelby!" Noah gasped.

"Did you find something?" Shelby stood up, her heart pounding with excitement.

"Sort of." Taking a cautious step backward, Noah spoke in a choked voice. "They're not killer bees, but—"

Shelby inhaled sharply as Noah suddenly sprayed the hanging plants with water from the canister. The harmless shower only served to enrage a mass of honeybees foraging in the flowers for nectar. Even though the two kids were wearing protective suits, instinct triggered an immediate reaction.

"Run!" Noah yelled as the mini-buzz-bombs swooped down on them.

Shelby ran. *Maybe Cindi's having better luck,* she hoped.

Cindi paused to study her reflection in Jason's front window before knocking. The shades were drawn and he couldn't see out. Her short, curly hair was stuffed under a brimmed hat she wore canted at a slight angle. Combined with the tailored white blouse, dark pants and jacket she had borrowed from her mom's closet, the outfit made her look chic and professional. Sunglasses and a grim expression completed the business-like impression she had strived to create. She was pretty sure Jason wouldn't recognize her. Squaring her shoulders and lifting her chin, Cindi rapped on the door.

"What *is* it?" Throwing open the door, Jason looked and sounded annoyed at the interruption.

"Are you Jason Hopkins?" The hint of a cultured European accent Cindi had practiced on the drive over came out just right. She would have smiled except it was totally out of character.

"Yeah." Jason frowned cautiously, then blinked. "Aren't you Shelby Woo's friend?"

Cindi smiled. So she wasn't a master of disguise. It had been fun trying to fool the artist, but luckily, her cover story didn't depend on hiding her identity.

"Yes, I am. Cindi Ornette. My uncle Phil owns the Horizon Art Center." Cindi calmly handed him the business card she had fabricated on her dad's computer. "I'm working part-time for him this summer, looking for new and talented artists that need gallery exposure. Shelby just loves your work and suggested that I stop by."

"The Horizon Art Center, huh?" A flicker of interest flashed across Jason's face as he took the card. "This isn't a joke, is it?"

"No. Not at all." Cindi ignored a sudden twinge of guilt. She could tell Jason didn't quite believe a gallery was interested in his work—yet he desperately wanted to. She'd save feeling bad about it until *after* she knew if he was or wasn't the tourist robber. "Can I see your work? Alone, if you wouldn't mind?"

Jason hesitated, giving her a questioning gaze. "It's just that I'll be too distracted to get a true emotional impact from your paintings if you're staring over my shoulder." Cindi shrugged apologetically.

"I paint sailing ships."

"Exactly." Cindi risked glancing at him over the top of her glasses. "I love sailing ships."

"All right. But only because you're Shelby's friend." Jason waved her inside. "Excuse the mess. This place isn't very big, I'm afraid."

I'll say! Cindi thought privately as she stepped through the door. The bungalow had one large room that served as a combination living room, bedroom and studio. An arched doorway led into the kitchen. Jason's furniture consisted of a hide-a-bed, a dresser, a table and two chairs. Paintings, blank canvases, art supplies, matting materials, clothes and construction tools were stacked and scattered everywhere. Finding a few wallets, watches and credit cards would not be easy. *Maybe impossible*, Cindi thought dismally.

Jason stepped out onto the porch. "Your uncle Phil really owns the Horizon Art Center?"

"Yes, he does." Cindi smiled and closed the door. That, at least, was not a lie. In fact, if Jason's paintings were as good as Shelby thought they were, her uncle might really be interested

in showing them. His tourist clientele loved anything with a Florida theme.

Hidden from view by the drawn shades, Cindi
began to move from painting to painting, flipping through them. The canvases were stretched
over wooden frames. There was plenty of space
to hide the small pieces of evidence behind them.
Nothing. She poked through the supplies and
looked in the dresser drawers, which Jason had
conveniently left open. The drawers were empty.
Most of his clothes were piled on the floor. Nothing fell out of the folds or pockets when she
shook them. Nothing was tucked under the thin
hide-a-bed mattress, either—including the
sheets. The kitchen sink was filled with dirty
dishes. The refrigerator and the cupboards were
bare. Judging from the overflowing trash can,
Jason ate out or brought fast food in.

Stepping out the door, Cindi swept past Jason
without stopping. "I'm *very* impressed. I'm
going to tell Uncle Phil to be sure and catch your
display at the art show!"

And that's the honest truth, Cindi thought as
she strode purposefully down the walk without
looking back. Her uncle would be impressed,
too. Jason's paintings were beautifully executed
with an attention to detail that made the sailing

ships come alive. She was sure he'd be a financially successful artist someday—if he wasn't sent to jail for robbing tourists. The fact that she hadn't found a stolen wallet or credit card in Jason's house wasn't conclusive proof that he was innocent. Still, Shelby would be relieved. Cindi didn't have to be a super sleuth to know that her best friend really liked the young artist.

Jumping into her old blue convertible, Cindi turned the key and held her breath as the motor sputtered, then started. She wasn't nearly as eager to tackle the next phase of Shelby's investigation as she had been to impersonate an art agent.

The next phase was Cory Conrad.

"No way, Shelby!" Sitting in the backseat of Cindi's car, Noah crossed his arms and shook his head. "Being chased by a bunch of kamikaze bees is one thing. Tangling with Cory is another."

Shelby turned sideways in the passenger seat and stared at him. It was Thursday, and except for knowing that all three suspects had opportunity and motive, they hadn't even put a dent in the case. Without hard evidence that connected someone else to the robberies, the shroud of suspicion would continue to hang over Will.

Cory Conrad was their last chance.

"All you have to do is *talk* to him, Noah." Cindi turned right into a wealthy neighborhood. "Shelby and I are the ones who'll be taking the real risk."

"But we can't search his room without *your* help." Shelby's dark-eyed stare was fixed on Noah. He was constantly trying to squirm out of her schemes to collect evidence, but eventually he always gave in. "If we don't do this, Will's life might be ruined."

"All right!" Exhaling loudly, Noah threw up his hands. "But I'm not gonna like it."

Cindi smiled and winked at Shelby as she parked by the curb. Piling out of the car, they peered through a thick hedge lining the Conrad property. Cory's red sports car was parked at the top of the curved drive by the front door.

"Are you sure nobody's home but Cory?" Noah asked nervously.

Shelby nodded. "I called and offered to demonstrate a new miracle cosmetic that prevents and removes wrinkles. The housekeeper told me any day would be fine—except Thursday. Mrs. Conrad does volunteer work at the hospital and it's her day off."

"Just my luck," Noah muttered.

Cindi squeezed his shoulder. "Look at it as an excellent opportunity to test just how good an actor you really are!"

"That's right, Noah," Shelby said. "Cory's front porch is just another stage."

"Except I'll be auditioning for a trip to the hospital!" Noah shuddered.

Shelby gave him a thumbs-up. "You're on."

Sighing, Noah trudged up the circular driveway. Slipping through the hedge, Shelby and Cindi used the dense, tropical gardens as cover. They arrived at the side of the sprawling, one-story house as Noah rang the bell.

Cory opened the door and growled, "Whatever you're selling, we don't want any!"

Noah jammed his foot in the door before Cory could slam it closed, pleading, "Wait! I'm desperate and you're the only person who can help me!"

Shelby motioned Cindi to follow as she moved toward the sliding glass doors by a side patio.

"Yeah?" Cory paused suspiciously. "Who says?"

"Uh . . . Jason Hopkins. I, uh . . . need five hundred dollars by this afternoon or I'm in big trouble!"

The glass door wasn't locked, and the girls eased silently inside.

"What for?" Cory asked.

"The cops!" Noah said with breathless anxiety. "They impounded my dad's car 'cause I parked it in front of a fire hydrant, and I've got to get it back!"

Moving soundlessly across a luxuriant carpet, Shelby and Cindi scurried down a long hallway. Cory was an only child, and his room was easy to locate.

One thing is certain, Shelby realized as they entered, leaving the door ajar like they found it. *Cory has expensive tastes.* The stereo, computer, TV and VCR were state-of-the-art. His books were leather-bound, not paperbacks, and all the latest electronic games were neatly stacked on a shelf. Either his father gave him everything he wanted or his loan-sharking business was booming.

Or Cory was a thief.

Another sliding glass door led out to the pool. It was open, too. *A handy escape route if we need it,* Shelby thought as she and Cindi began searching opposite sides of the immaculate room. Everything was in perfect order. Cory didn't have a junk drawer or shoe boxes stuffed with odds and ends in his closet. There wasn't even any dust under the bed. If the stolen goods were hidden in Cory's room, they were stashed behind a secret panel.

And Shelby didn't have time to look for one.

"Stupid waste of time!" Cory shouted as he stormed down the hall.

Cindi ran out through the glass door.

Stuck between the wall and the bed, Shelby was trapped. She flattened herself on the floor a split second before Cory came in and slammed the door.

"Hopkins had no business sending *anyone* to me for money!" Fuming, Cory paced back and forth. "Especially a loser like *that* guy!"

Shelby cringed as she peered out from under the bed and watched his sneakered feet. She had no doubt that if Cory Conrad caught her, he would call the police. If she accused him of being a loan shark, he would deny it and the police would probably believe him. His father, Clayton Conrad, was a rich and influential man in the community.

Then an even more horrible realization hit her.

If she was arrested for breaking and entering, her dreams of becoming an official police detective would be shattered forever!

Chapter
7

Shelby swallowed a gasp as Cory suddenly stopped moving. Did he know she was there?

A flood of repeated warnings rushed into her mind. Her grandfather and Detective Hineline had told her over and over again to keep her inquisitive nose out of police business before she got into serious trouble. For one brief, fleeting moment, Shelby wished she had listened.

A girl laughed outside.

Cindi? Shelby tensed.

"Hey!" Cory leaped toward the glass door.

Shelby heard a huge splash and the glass door being pushed aside as Cory rushed out. She crawled to the end of the bed.

"What do you think you're doing?" Cory demanded.

"Cooling off!" Cindi laughed again. "It's a scorcher today!"

Through the open door, Shelby saw Cindi treading water in Cory's pool. Her daring friend had jumped in with her clothes on to create a diversion so she could escape! Way to go, Cindi!

"Out!" Cory screamed. "Get out!"

Cindi shrugged, then leisurely dog-paddled to the edge of the pool.

There was nothing leisurely about Shelby's dash for freedom. Darting across the floor on her hands and knees, she scooted out of the bedroom. She was on her feet and running for the front door the instant she hit the hall. She was outside in ten seconds flat.

Squatting by the corner of the garage, Noah waved her to run on.

Shelby ran, glancing over her shoulder. Neither Cindi nor Cory was in sight. Noah reached into a cabinet filled with pipes and valves that was attached to the garage. As Shelby ducked behind a neighbor's hedge, he turned the valves, then raced down the drive. Dripping wet, Cindi sprinted around the house and toward the road. Cory ran after her, waving his arms and shouting. He skidded to a surprised halt as the lawn sprinklers suddenly came on. Noah zoomed past Shelby. Cindi put on an extra burst of speed. Disoriented by the unexpected shower, Cory gave up the chase.

"Let's go! Let's go!" Cindi urged Shelby as she rounded the end of the hedge.

Shelby raced after her for the car. Noah was already in the driver's seat with the motor running. A second after both girls dove into the backseat of the old convertible, he hit the gas.

As usual on a Friday night, C.J.'s was bustling. Shelby, Cindi and Noah sat across the street from the burger joint in Cindi's car. The top was up to provide cover.

Shelby checked her watch. *Almost eleven.* Will, Jason and Linda were working inside. Cory hadn't shown up, yet.

"Squad car alert!" Noah hissed.

They all ducked until the police cruiser passed. Shelby didn't want to be spotted staking out a crime scene. Detective Hineline would be totally ticked-off if he found out she was investigating. The three kids had been lucky the previous afternoon. Shelby had checked all the new crime reports at the station and seen that Cory hadn't called the police to report a break-in or Cindi's trespassing.

"My neck is starting to ache from all this ducking." Cindi rubbed the sore muscles and moaned as she sat up.

"And I'm getting hungry," Noah said.

The flow of customers was slowing down, so Shelby decided it was probably safe to go in. They could hang out for an hour until closing without appearing obvious.

Shelby nodded. "Okay. I could use a soda myself."

The outside table closest to the door was empty and they grabbed it. Linda dropped three menus in front of them as she walked by to take an order.

Noah paled suddenly. "Cory's coming."

Simultaneously, all three raised the menus to hide their faces. Shelby peeked over the top of hers as Cory marched past and went inside. The kids at Cory's favorite table were getting up to leave. He sat down in the first vacated chair, shoving their empty baskets and cups aside.

"I don't like this plan, Shelby." Noah glanced inside as Will brought Cory a soda. "We won't be there to help if Cory catches you following him."

"We don't have a choice," Shelby interrupted. She had given considerable thought to the robber's method of operation. The thief didn't drive away. Whoever it was lurked around C.J.'s on foot, waiting for a likely victim. "There are three suspects and three of us. Cory saw both of you yesterday. He *didn't* see me."

"But he warned *you* to stay out of his business last week at Jason's," Cindi reminded her.

"That was last week and I was visiting Jason. I wasn't asking Cory for money or taking an uninvited swim in his pool. Besides, if he just drives away, that'll be the end of it." Shelby hesitated, frowning.

"What are you thinking?" Cindi sat back slightly.

Shelby shrugged. "With all these extra patrol cars driving around, I don't think the robber will strike again tonight. The odds of getting nabbed are too great."

"So why are we bothering to tail anyone?"

"Just in case, Noah," Shelby answered. "Just in case."

Noah raised his menu to hide his face again. "Peter's on the deck."

Shielding her face with her hand, Cindi turned away and pretended to read her menu.

Shelby glanced back, as though trying to get Linda's attention. It was very unlikely Peter would identify her as one of the Health Department people who had shown up to inspect his house for killer bees.

"The car's parked in the side lot, Linda." Peter stopped his sister on her way back to the door.

Balancing a stack of empty baskets on one arm, Linda took the car keys Peter held out and stuffed them in her jeans pocket. "Do I have enough gas to get home?"

"I filled it up. Gotta run." Peter turned to leave. "See you later!"

Shelby quickly turned back to her menu.

"Be with you guys in a minute," Linda said as she hurried inside. She didn't even look at them.

Cindi's eyes lit up. "It would be kinda hard to make a fast getaway if there wasn't any gas in the car."

"Exactly what I was thinking." Pushing her menu aside, Shelby settled back. All the players were in place, and there was nothing to do now but wait.

Forty-five minutes later, the last few customers began to pay their bills and leave. Linda cleared and cleaned the outside tables with hurried efficiency. Cory waved a five-dollar bill, trying to get Will's attention.

"Time to get in position." Rising, Shelby started to climb over the bench and froze. Cindi and Noah paused halfway out of their seats.

"Thought I'd find you here, Shelby." Planting himself in front of her, Hineline fixed Shelby with a knowing stare.

"Well, I hang out here a lot." Shelby nodded and smiled. "But it's getting late and we've gotta get going."

"Sit." Hineline pointed to the table, then at Cindi and Noah. "You, too."

They all sank back into their seats as Cory rushed past. He vanished around the corner of the building before Shelby could mutter a protest.

"But—"

"No buts, Shelby," Hineline ordered. "I don't know what you've been up to concerning this tourist robbery case, but you're not going to interfere in police operations tonight. Is that clear?"

Shelby nodded, then sighed as Cory's red car drove out of the parking lot and turned right.

"Good." Gripping the table, Hineline leaned toward Shelby to make sure she understood. "Just sit there and be quiet until I get back."

Through the front window, Shelby saw Will hoist a trash bag. He left through the back door to dump it. Linda checked all the equipment to make sure it was turned off. Then Jason closed the door and locked it from inside. A moment later all the lights went out.

"I can't say I'm sorry Detective Hineline stopped us from going through with our plan," Noah mumbled.

"I am." Cindi rested her chin on her crossed arms. "I was looking forward to tailing Linda."

"We would have been wasting our time." Shelby scowled as Jason's car turned right onto the street behind Linda. The artist was headed toward the bank to make the night deposit as usual, but Linda was going in the opposite direction of her house. "None of our suspects are hanging around. Too many cops."

Hineline's loud voice carried from the parking lot, breaking the late-night silence. "What do you mean 'you lost him'?"

"Lost who?" Cindi whispered.

Shelby shrugged and strained to listen. She couldn't see much in the dark.

"I hung back so he wouldn't spot me when he came out with the trash," an officer explained. "Then the lights went out. He disappeared in the dark before I could track him. Guess it wasn't his turn to lock up."

"Great." Squinting into the glare of a patrol car's headlights, Hineline stepped back as Tracy Mendoza pulled up. "Anything?"

"No, sir," Mendoza reported. "All the customers are gone. No one approached any of them."

Shelby leaned over the table and whispered, "That's something to be grateful for."

"Yeah," Noah agreed. "As long as the police are out in force, the streets are safe for tourists again."

"More than that," Shelby said. "Even though we're no closer to proving Will is innocent, the police aren't any closer to proving he's guilty, either."

As Mendoza drove off with the other officer, Hineline waved at Shelby. "Come on. I'll drive you home."

"Be right there!" Rising, Shelby explained, "I might as well go with him. Maybe he knows something we don't."

Noah eased off the bench and yawned as Cindi fished her keys out of her pocket. Detective Hineline insisted on waiting until they were safely on their way. Then he led Shelby to an unmarked police car in the parking lot.

"So what are you going to do now?" Shelby asked as she scooted into the front seat.

"Take you home, then get some sleep." Hineline started the engine. "And I'm not going to answer any more of your questions."

"Oh." Sighing, Shelby stared out the window as the detective turned right onto the empty street. Fighting off a sense of despair, she watched the darkened windows of office buildings and closed shops whiz by. *He probably doesn't* know *what to do next*, she decided. *I sure don't!*

"Stop!" Shelby shouted out, craning her neck to look out the back window.

Hineline slammed on the brakes, and said in a resigned tone, "Now what, Shelby?"

"I saw someone lying on the ground by the bank!"

Frowning, Hineline whipped a police light onto the top of the car and turned it on. Then he shifted and backed up.

"There!" Shelby pointed.

A woman dragged herself into a sitting position under the dimly lit, drive-up overhang. She was wearing jeans, and her dark hair was tied back. Spotting the strobing red light, she waved and cried out, "Help! I've been robbed!"

Shelby gasped. The victim was Linda Alvarez!

Chapter
8

Shelby hovered on the edge of the crime scene, taking in every little detail. The street was dark and three of the four lights in the bank drive-up area were burned out. Tracy Mendoza and another uniformed officer were keeping everyone clear of the area until forensics arrived to search for evidence. Linda's car was also significantly absent.

"You've only got a couple of minor abrasions," a rescue worker assured Linda. "Nothing to worry about."

"The thief just pushed me down and grabbed the bag. He didn't hit me or anything." Linda took a deep breath, calmer now that the police and paramedics had arrived.

"Did you see the person who attacked you?"
Detective Hineline asked.

"No. He came up behind me and—*wham*—I
was on the ground. It all happened so fast."

The detective jotted a note on his pad. "Do
you usually make the bank deposit after C.J.'s
closes, Ms. Alvarez?"

Linda shook her head. "No, Jason Hopkins
does. He's the weekend night manager. But he
had something important to do, so I volunteered
to drop the bag instead."

What was so important that Jason couldn't
take a few minutes to make the bank deposit?
Shelby wondered, shivering. Maybe *stealing* the
bank deposit?

She instantly recalled Jason's conversation
with Cory Conrad last Saturday afternoon.

"I don't want your appreciation," Cory
sneered. "I want my thousand bucks."

Jason nodded patiently. "And you'll get it.
Next Saturday afternoon at three. Just like we
agreed."

"It'll be twelve hundred next Saturday. And
you'd better have all of it or else!" Cory shook
his fist in Jason's face.

"Or else what?"

"Or else I'm going to punch holes in your precious paintings." Cory lunged at the nearest canvas with a huge nail. Jason jumped to stop him, but Cory stopped himself—just short of shoving the four-inch spike through a picture of a two-masted sailboat. . . .

Jason had to pay Cory twelve hundred dollars tomorrow afternoon!

Shelby suddenly felt empty inside. As much as she liked and admired the young artist, she couldn't deny the facts. If Jason didn't settle the debt on time, Cory would destroy his beautiful paintings. Jason desperately needed a lot of money in a hurry. *But is he desperate enough to steal C.J.'s Friday night earnings?*

Frowning, Shelby mentally filed the incriminating information about Jason and stepped into the circle of people surrounding Linda. There was another important factor that no one had noticed or bothered to ask about.

"Did the thief steal your car, too?" Shelby asked.

"No—" Linda started to answer.

"I told *you* to stay in the car!" Hineline glared at Shelby, then blinked as he looked back at

Linda. "I thought you walked up to the deposit drop box."

"I did. I left my car about two blocks back because I had a flat tire." Linda shook her head. "If I had been driving, this probably wouldn't have happened."

"Not necessarily," Shelby pointed out. "With the lights out, the thief could have hidden in the shadows, then jumped out and snatched the bag right out of your hand before you had a chance to drop it in the box."

"Are you finished?" Hineline asked sarcastically.

"Yes. Am I right?"

"Yes, but that's beside the point—"

"Detective Hineline!" Officer Mendoza's flashlight was trained on the ground where Linda had been attacked.

Hanging back so Hineline wouldn't give her a direct order to return to the car, Shelby watched as the detective took a white handkerchief out of his pocket.

Stooping, Hineline used the cloth to pick something up. "Looks like our tourist robber decided to go after something more profitable than a wallet tonight."

Shelby's eyes widened in alarm.

Detective Hineline was holding a C.J.'s pen.

Shelby rode quietly in the backseat of the un-marked car. Linda had insisted on going home rather than to the hospital, and Detective Hine-line had insisted on dropping the shaken robbery victim off first. That was fine with Shelby. She had a lot to think about.

Foremost on her mind was the C.J.'s pen. Find-ing it at the bank had convinced Hineline that the same person who had been attacking tourists had stolen the bank bag. He didn't say so, but she knew Will was still his primary suspect. To make matters worse, it looked as if Will had slipped away in the dark after C.J.'s closed so he wouldn't be tailed. Shelby could only hope that someone had seen him somewhere else at the time Linda was robbed.

Besides, Shelby mused, *the pen could belong to anyone.* Customers and everyone who worked at C.J.'s used them. Linda still had a pen in her back pocket, but like Will, who was always for-getting the pens he tucked over his ears, she might have had a second pen. And that pen might have fallen out of her pocket when she was shoved to the ground.

Forensics will know for sure by tomorrow morning, Shelby thought as Hineline pulled into Linda's driveway. Fingerprints would positively ID the pen's owner.

"I'll help you to the door," Hineline said as he stepped out of the car. "You stay here, Shelby."

Shelby paused as she reached for her door handle.

"No, please. Let her come in," Linda said. "I know it's late, but my younger brother is probably waiting up for me and I'd like to introduce them. Peter doesn't know any of the kids in town yet."

"Suit yourself." Hineline shrugged.

Shelby didn't say anything as she walked behind them to the door. She didn't want to push her luck.

Peter was lounging on the sofa watching TV. He kept his eyes on the screen as he casually flipped through the channels. "Hi, Sis. What took you so long?"

"I, uh . . . was robbed. At the bank."

The remote dropped from Peter's hand as he sat up and stared at Linda. The blood drained from his face. "You were—"

"Don't worry," Linda said quickly. "I'm all

right. Detective Hineline and Shelby were driving by—"

Peter's head snapped around. "They saw it happen?"

"I'm afraid not," Hineline said. "The thief was gone when we arrived."

Nodding, Peter jumped up and rushed to help Linda to the couch. "Are you sure you're not hurt?"

The strain of the night's events finally caught up with Linda. Collapsing on the sofa, she began to cry softly. "Sometimes you just can't win," she said between sniffles. "Peter finally remembers to put gas in the car so I won't have to stop on my way home like I have been on Fridays and what happens? I get a flat tire. I have to walk to the bank and—somebody *robs* me!"

"A flat?" Peter frowned. "The tire was fine when I parked the car."

"She probably ran over a nail or something on the road," Hineline said.

Shelby studied the distressed young woman. She had not dismissed the possibility that Linda had faked the robbery and stashed the bank bag in her car. However, stopping for gas would explain why Linda had gotten home so late the past three Fridays. If her story checked out,

Linda had an alibi for the time of the tourist attacks outside C.J.'s.

Sniffling back her tears, Linda grabbed Peter's arm. "You've got to go change the tire and bring the car back—tonight. I can't afford a service call or a ticket."

Shelby kept her expression impassive, but her mind was racing. Linda's reasoning made sense considering her financial troubles. Still, she was awfully anxious to get the car back as soon as possible.

"You won't get a ticket," Hineline assured her.

"I'll go get the car anyway." Peter fondly patted Linda's shoulder. "It'll make you feel better, right?"

Linda nodded.

"I'll drive you back," Hineline offered.

Peter hesitated, then shrugged. "Yeah, sure. Just let me grab some tools and I'll be right with you."

Shelby couldn't help but notice that Peter seemed less than enthusiastic about accepting a ride from the detective. But then, she reminded herself, the police made a lot of kids nervous even when they hadn't done anything wrong.

This time, Peter sat in the backseat holding a backpack full of tools. Hineline drove in silence.

Remembering the track trophies Noah had seen, Shelby easily engaged Peter in a friendly conversation about his favorite sport.

"Dropping the baton in my first relay race was pretty embarrassing." Peter gripped the piece of cylindrical wood he kept in his backpack. Shelby remembered it from the day of the bee inspection.

"I'll bet," Shelby agreed.

"But it's never happened again. Linda helps me practice handing off, and I carry this when I run my miles." Peter stuffed the relay baton in the front pocket of the backpack. "I was the anchor on the team at my old school."

"I'm sure the track coach at Space Coast High will be glad to see you," Shelby said.

By the time they reached the car, the boy was relaxed and laughing, which made Shelby's plan a snap to implement. She knew this opportunity might be the only one she'd get to search the car. When Shelby offered to help with the tire and Peter agreed to drive her home, Hineline gave in with very little argument.

"Make sure it's in park, will you, Shelby?" Peter took a flashlight out of his backpack and handed it to her. He opened the trunk as Shelby moved to the front of the car.

Jumping into the driver's seat, Shelby glanced at the gearshift indicator and called out, "It's in park!"

"Okay. Thanks." Putting the backpack in the trunk, Peter pulled out the spare tire and jack.

Shelby took a moment to run her hand under the front seats. No bag. As she was about to slide out, she saw a credit card receipt on the floor and turned the flashlight beam on the paper. The date and time were clearly printed on a receipt from Corner Gas & Auto Repair. Linda had been pumping gas when Harold Wangler was robbed.

Which leaves only two possible suspects, Shelby thought glumly. *Jason and Cory.*

"I need you to hold the light for me!" Peter shouted.

"Coming!" Sighing, Shelby went to the back of the car. Leaning on the rear fender, she held the flashlight beam on the flat tire. She glanced at the backpack lying on a pile of old magazines, dirty rags, empty oil containers and assorted auto parts in the trunk. "Want me to get your other tools?"

Ignoring the question, Peter sat back on his heels. "Would you look at that!"

"What?" Curious, Shelby squatted to look.

"This!" Peter pointed to a huge nail in the

sidewall of the tire. "Linda couldn't have picked it up on the street, Shelby."

Shelby frowned with instant understanding. If Linda had run over the nail, it would be stuck where the tire made contact with the road—not in the side.

"Someone jammed this into her tire on purpose," Peter murmured.

"So she'd have to walk to the bank," Shelby quickly surmised. Even though it would have been possible for the robber to snatch the bag from someone in a car, grabbing it from someone on foot was infinitely easier.

"Kind of looks that way, doesn't it?" Getting a pair of pliers from the trunk, Peter yanked the nail free and handed it to Shelby.

Shelby's spirits sank as she stared at the four-inch spike. No amount of wishful thinking could alter the conclusion the evidence was forcing her to accept.

She wasn't positive, but the nail looked very much like those in Jason's carpenter's apron.

Jason needed twelve hundred dollars tomorrow.

And he was the only person who knew that earlier that night Linda was taking the restaurant deposit to the bank. . . .

Except maybe for Will.

Chapter
9

"You're awfully quiet this morning, Shelby." Mike Woo took a stack of dirty breakfast dishes from his granddaughter. "Is something wrong?"

Shelby shrugged and began loading the dishwasher while her grandfather rinsed. It was Saturday morning, and there were a lot of dishes because of weekend guests. "Did you ever solve a case that ended with a friend being guilty?" she asked her grandfather.

"Once. It was very difficult, but he was very guilty." Mike continued to scrub. "But catching the bad guys is what crime solving is all about, even when the bad guy is a friend."

Shelby just nodded. Her grandfather was right,

but that didn't make the situation any easier to handle. She had set out to prove one friend was innocent. Now she was almost positive another friend was guilty. She still didn't have conclusive evidence that Jason was the tourist robber, but everything was starting to point that way.

"So what case are you investigating now?" Mike looked Shelby in the eye as he held out a handful of dripping silverware.

"Me? Case? None. I was just curious." Shelby glanced at the wall clock. "Gotta run or I'll be late!"

Grabbing her shoulder bag, Shelby dashed out before her grandfather asked a direct question she couldn't evade. Although he was proud of her ability to solve difficult cases, he still worried about her. Too often following a trail of clues led her into danger. *But,* she thought as she flew out the door, *being in danger would almost be better than finding out someone I really like is a crook.*

Rushing into the station, Shelby went straight to Hineline's desk to hand over her evidence. By itself, the nail didn't prove anything. Every hardware store in town probably sold them. Even so, she had information regarding other possible suspects that her superior wasn't aware of. Combined, the nail and her suspicions might convince Hineline to consider the possibility that someone besides Will was robbing tourists and stealing bank bags.

But the detective wasn't at his desk.

"Where's Detective Hineline?" Shelby asked an officer passing by.

"He got a warrant to search Will Potter's house. He left about five minutes ago."

"A warrant?" Shelby blinked. "On the basis of what evidence?"

"The kid's fingerprints were the only ones on the pen Mendoza found at the crime scene. The lab got a positive match from a set they lifted off the trash can lid at C.J.'s. Guess Potter's the only one who ever takes out the garbage."

Turning on her heels, Shelby raced out of the building. In spite of the fingerprints, nothing could make her believe Will was guilty. There had to be a reasonable explanation. Only one came to mind. Linda or Jason had picked up one of Will's pens during the rush at C.J.'s last night, and one of them had dropped it at the bank. Obviously, Detective Hineline had also thought of that scenario. Will's fingerprints were enough to justify searching his house, but they weren't sufficient evidence for an arrest.

Hineline was on the front porch, speaking

with Will's parents, when Shelby arrived at the Potters'.

"We didn't get home until after two last night," Mr. Potter said to the detective.

"Will was here when we got in, though," Will's mom added anxiously.

Not good enough, Shelby thought as she paused behind Hineline. The bank bag was stolen shortly after midnight.

"I have a warrant to search the house." Hineline handed a folded paper to Will's dad, then glanced down at Shelby and asked, "What are *you* doing here?"

"After you left last night, I stumbled across something that might be important to this case."

"Will it melt?" Hineline asked.

Shelby shook her head. "No—"

"Then it'll wait." Hineline turned back to Will's parents, his tone softening. "I know how upset you folks must be, but I really have to get started."

Sighing as he scanned the warrant, Mr. Potter gestured for Hineline to enter the house. After the detective disappeared inside, Potter drew his wife aside. "I'm sure this is all some awful mistake."

"So am I," Shelby said. "I'm a friend of Will's

and I think I can help him. Do you mind if I go in?" Hineline couldn't keep her out if Will's parents gave her permission to enter, she figured.

"No, please. Anything to help Will," the distraught woman said.

"Thanks." Hearing noises upstairs, Shelby dashed to the second floor and down the hall. She stopped abruptly by the open door into Will's room, her eyes widening with disbelief as she peered around Detective Hineline.

Will was standing by his bed holding a sneaker in one hand and a C.J.'s bank bag in the other.

"Where did you get that bag, Will?" the detective asked.

"I got it from under my bed, but I don't know how it got there." Totally bewildered, Will shook his head. "There's a bunch of other stuff that doesn't belong to me, either. I was just looking for my shoes."

Spotting Shelby, Hineline waved her inside, then handed her his handkerchief and a plastic evidence bag. "As long as you're here, make yourself useful. Look under the bed."

Under any other circumstances, Shelby would have been thrilled to be part of an official investigation. But, as she carefully retrieved three wallets and three watches from under Will's bed, she was just numb. Finding the bank bag and the wallets together left no doubt that the same person had robbed the tourists and Linda.

Hineline's expression hardened. "Will, you're under arrest for assault and robbery. Anything you say may—"

Stunned, Shelby retreated into her own thoughts as the detective advised the boy of his rights. Even though they had caught him redhanded with the evidence, she still didn't believe Will was the robber. She was missing something that would explain everything, but she didn't have a clue what that something was.

But I do have a clue! she realized suddenly.

"Wait a minute," she said to the detective. Opening her purse, Shelby pulled out a plastic sandwich bag containing the nail. "I think whoever robbed Linda at the bank used this to flatten her tire." She held it out to him. "It's evidence."

"That's not evidence, Shelby." Hineline glanced at the nail, raised a skeptical eyebrow, then held up the bag with the stolen wallets and watches. *"This* is evidence."

Shelby had worked for Hineline long enough

to know it was futile to argue. She touched Will's arm. "Don't give up, Will. This isn't over yet."

"I really don't care, Shelby," Will said in a dejected voice. "Linda stood me up."

"Let's go." Hineline led Will out of the room.

"What do you mean 'Linda stood you up'?" Hard on Will's heels, Shelby latched onto the comment like a drowning man grabs onto a life preserver. "When did *you* have a date with *Linda?*"

"Last night. She called and asked me to meet her at the park, but she didn't show. Some joke, huh? I know she wasn't feeling well, but—" Hanging his head, Will sighed.

Did Will know Linda was upset about being robbed? Shelby frowned, phrasing her next question carefully. "Did she say that? That she wasn't feeling well?"

"No. She just sounded funny."

"What time did she call?" Shelby asked, hiding her excitement.

"About quarter after one, I guess. What difference does it make?"

"None," Hineline said as he urged Will to move ahead of him down the stairs.

Wrong, Shelby thought triumphantly as she followed them to Hineline's car. Somebody pretending to be Linda had used Will's crush on the young woman to lure him out of the house. His parents hadn't gotten home until after two. The real thief had stashed the stolen goods under Will's bed while everyone was out.

Will had been set up.

Sitting at her desk at the station that afternoon, Shelby stared at the nail while the last few minutes of her shift dragged by.

"Outta here, Shelby," Hineline ordered. "Watching you study that nail is giving *me* eyestrain."

Grabbing the plastic bag, Shelby was out of her seat and gone without being told a second time. She was positive the nail was the key to solving the case, but Detective Hineline refused to give it any credence or listen to her theories about Jason.

Just as well, Shelby thought as she waited for Cindi and Noah on the sidewalk. She needed positive proof before she pointed the finger at another friend. Although it didn't seem likely, Jason just might be innocent, too.

"Where to?" Cindi asked as Shelby got into the backseat of the blue Ford.

"Jason's house." Shelby had briefed Cindi

about recent events on the phone during her break at the photo shop. "We've got to find out if this nail matches the ones in his carpenter's apron."

"I hope you've figured out how to get into his house again, because I'm fresh out of brilliant pretenses at the moment," Noah said.

"Easy." Shelby grinned. "Jason's at the sidewalk art show, so there's nobody home."

"Oh, well! Now all we have to worry about is getting caught breaking and entering and becoming Will's cellmates." Resting his elbow on the door, Noah propped his chin on his hand and sighed.

"I don't like sneaking into houses and poking around in people's stuff, either," Shelby said seriously. "But if we don't, Hineline could convict Will. He's got enough evidence."

"You don't think there's any chance Will really is guilty, do you?" Cindi asked hesitantly.

"None," Shelby said confidently.

"I don't think so, either, but I had to ask." Cindi pulled over in front of Jason's house.

Shelby jumped out first. "You two stay here. This will only take a minute."

Striding boldly up the walk, Shelby tried the door and found it unlocked. She walked inside without hesitating or looking around. If anyone *was* watching, her unconcerned demeanor and actions would look less suspicious. The apron was lying on the floor. Within a few seconds, Shelby knew that the bagged nail from Linda's tire was identical to those in the canvas pocket.

Facts are facts, Shelby told herself as she pocketed the plastic bag and headed for the door. She couldn't deny them no matter how much she wanted to. Making sure the door was securely latched, Shelby turned to leave. *Every time I turn around, Jason looks more and more guilty,* she thought grimly.

Except this time! Shelby's memory clicked as she stared at the protruding nail that had snagged her shirt. Hardly daring to hope, she ran back to the car.

"Didn't the nails match?" Cindi asked.

"Perfectly." Shelby grinned.

"Then how come you're so happy?" Cindi frowned. "That means Jason is still your number one suspect."

"Not necessarily."

Jason isn't the only suspect who had access to his carpenter's apron. Cory threatened to

puncture the paintings with one of Jason's own nails. . . .

Cory stopped himself just short of shoving the four-inch spike through a picture of a two-masted ketch under full-sail.

"You wouldn't dare!" Jason glared at the teenager.

"It's your decision, Hopkins. Get me the money, or the paintings are trashed." Pocketing the nail, Cory turned abruptly and charged for the door.

Cory took that nail with him when he left.

"So it could be either one of them," Noah concluded.

"Right." Shelby's brow furrowed in thought. "They both drove off in the same direction as Linda last night. And Cory's been hanging around C.J.'s long enough to know that Will has a desperate crush on Linda. Cory could have made the phony phone call to Linda."

"But Jason knows that, too," Cindi said. "And *he* knew Linda was taking the bank deposit."

"Cory didn't know that," Noah pointed out.

Shelby wasn't discouraged. "We don't know

that for sure. I didn't ask Linda what *time* she and Jason talked about changing places. Cory was the last customer to leave besides us. He could have overheard the conversation."

"So how do we find out?" Noah asked cautiously. *"I'm* not going to ask him."

"We don't have to." Shelby checked her watch. "We can just make it."

"Make it where?" Cindi put the car in gear.

"The art show by three o'clock," Shelby said as she settled back. "Either Jason has the money to pay back Cory's loan or he doesn't."

Chapter
10

Slinging her bag over her shoulder, Shelby studied the plaza sidewalk. The artists were set up in front of stores and around a small, central park. A huge crowd jammed the walkways and closed-off streets. "We've got to get moving if we're going to find Jason's display before three," she said to her two friends.

"I'm ready." Cindi's eyes sparkled with anticipation.

They started at one end of the block and worked their way around the square. Between fighting the crowd and pulling Cindi away from cute animal pictures that caught her eye, a half hour passed before they finally located Jason, at ten minutes to three.

As they approached his display, Shelby saw a man walk away with one of Jason's smaller paintings tucked under his arm. The artist counted through a wad of bills, then stuffed the roll back into his pocket.

Playing it safe, Cindi and Noah stopped at the booth next to Jason's. They wanted to stick close in case Shelby needed help, but they didn't want to attract Jason's attention unless it was necessary.

"Sofa art," Noah muttered as the artist at the booth, an elderly woman with flaming red hair, instantly went into her pitch. Her panels were covered with huge, framed paintings. All of them were versions of the same basic seascape done in different colors.

Cindi made a face as she studied the bland, generic seascapes. "They're okay for office lobbies, I guess, but I wouldn't hang one in my living room."

"Hey, Shelby!" Jason smiled and waved. "What brings you down here?"

"I came to see you," Shelby answered honestly. "How's it going?"

Like most of the other artists' setups, Jason's display was made of three pegboard panels with the longest one in back. Two shorter panels formed the sides. Jason's more expensive paintings hung on the panels. The smaller pictures were set in cardboard boxes that allowed browsers to flip through them.

"Not too bad, actually. I've sold a few small pieces, and a couple of other prospects promised to come back." Running his hand through his long hair, Jason took a deep breath. "Sure hope they do. One of them is an interior decorator who's redoing the lobby of the yacht club."

"I'm really glad for you, Jason." Shelby hid her darker thoughts behind a smile. She had to remember that if Jason *was* the tourist robber, not only was he a thug and a thief—he had framed Will.

Jason's eyes narrowed. "Do me a favor, will you, Shelby? Watch things for a minute."

Spotting Cory weaving his way through the crowd, Shelby nodded. Taking another deep breath and shaking his head, Jason stepped behind the side panel. Noting his worried expression, Shelby's heart fluttered. *Maybe Jason doesn't have the money!* she hoped.

Graciously fleeing the sofa artist, Cindi and Noah pretended to study Jason's work as Cory joined Jason behind the panel on the left. Shelby hovered on the opposite side, listening.

"It's three o'clock, Hopkins," Cory said in a cool voice.

"Here's three hundred. I need a couple more hours," Jason said.

"Tough! I've got a four-thirty collection from another sucker at the pier." Cory jabbed a finger into Jason's chest and continued, "You still owe me nine hundred dollars plus interest. I'm going to collect some of that *now!*"

"What are you—"

Shelby started as Cory charged around to the front of the panel with the nail from Jason's apron clutched between his fingers. Jason lunged after him but was stopped by a man passing by with a huge pink seascape balanced on his shoulder.

The furious loan shark sprang toward a large, spectacular painting of several sloops with raised spinnaker sails rounding a racing buoy.

Shelby had noticed the price tag and a "hold" sticker on the frame. The painting was a steal for nine hundred and fifty dollars, but it wouldn't be worth anything if Cory punched holes in it. She reached for Cory's shirt and missed.

"Nobody crosses me!" Cory drew his arm back, then plunged the nail toward the canvas.

In the same instant, Noah sidestepped as though admiring the painting from a different angle. He bumped into Cory, making him stumble.

The nail missed its target.

"Watch who you're shoving, jerk!" Glaring, Cory turned on Noah.

"It was an accident," Noah said, backing out of the display area with his hands raised. "Really!"

As Cory raised his arm, Jason grabbed his wrist. Prying the hostile boy's fingers open, the artist took the nail and growled, "This belongs to me."

"Mr. Hopkins?" A smartly dressed woman paused before the display, frowning uncertainly. A small, nervous-looking man stood by her side.

"Mrs. Anthony! I'll be right with you!" Jason's bright smile of greeting faded as he backed Cory up against the side panel. "Don't move, Conrad. Or else."

"I think he means it, Cory," Shelby said as Jason hurried to take care of his customer.

"Who asked you?" Cory scowled sullenly, but he didn't move.

Shelby just shrugged and watched as Jason removed the spinnaker painting. The small man

106

beamed with delight as he handed over the selling price in cash. Jason pocketed fifty and gave Cory the nine hundred dollars he still owed.

"And by the way," Jason said as Cory pushed past him. "Stay out of C.J.'s. You're banned."

"Big deal." Seething, Cory rudely elbowed his way through the throng of people passing by.

Shelby frowned as Cindi scurried into the crowd behind him. *What's she up to?* A second later, Noah moved out after Cindi. Catching Shelby's eye, he motioned for her to follow them. Shelby nodded. First she wanted to talk to Jason while he was alone.

"That guy is such a jerk." Jason shook his head. "Cory's interest rates are bad enough, but the power trip he gets from pushing people around is worse. I should never have borrowed money from him."

"Why did you?" Shelby asked, pretending not to know.

"To get into this show." An embarrassed flush blossomed on Jason's cheeks. "A stupid thing to do, huh?"

"Taking money from Cory? Yes." Shelby smiled. "But getting your work seen by all these people? I don't think so. And you sold some paintings, too."

"That was a reckless gamble. I couldn't have paid Cory if Mr. Anthony hadn't bought 'Spinnaker Glory.' "

"Well, at least things seem to be working out okay."

"More than you know." Jason grinned. "Last night after work I had coffee with a gallery rep from Palm Beach. There's a good chance I'll get a one-man show sometime in the next few months."

"Not just a chance, Mr. Hopkins." A young, impeccably groomed man in a three-piece suit stepped forward. "I spoke to the gallery owner last night after we finished talking. Woke him out of a sound sleep at one-forty A.M." He reached inside his jacket and pulled out a white paper. "Sign this contract and you'll be our featured artist in October."

Shelby slipped away. Jason was too excited to notice, but she didn't mind. He had worked hard for his big break and he wasn't a criminal. With seven hundred dollars in stolen tourist money and the C.J.'s receipts, Jason would have had more than enough to pay Cory without selling a single picture. In addition, he had a confirmed alibi. Jason was with the art agent when Linda was robbed. And they were still having coffee when the robber planted the wallets and watches in Will's room.

Which left Cory.

Heading out in the direction her friends had taken, Shelby mentally reviewed all their evidence against the teenaged loan shark. She hadn't really scrutinized the case from the Cory angle because things had looked so bad for Jason. She suddenly realized that they didn't have *anything* that positively linked Jason to the crimes.

After searching for fifteen minutes, Shelby finally found Noah crouched behind a parked car on a side street. Up ahead, Cindi was lounging against Cory's red sports car, talking and laughing with him.

"What's she doing?" Shelby whispered.

"Apologizing to Cory for jumping in his pool," Noah said calmly. "And pretending she did it to get his attention."

"What?" Shelby's mouth fell open. "Why?"

"So maybe he'll brag about robbing tourists or something."

Hearing Cindi laugh, Shelby looked up to see her wave as Cory drove away. Cindi wasn't laughing when she started walking back.

"I don't know how to tell you this, Noah,

but . . ." Shelby sighed. "I don't think Cory did it."

"What makes you say that?" Noah was stunned.

"For one thing," Shelby explained glumly, "he still had the nail he took from Jason. He didn't jam it into Linda's sidewall."

"Well, maybe the nail in Linda's tire was just a freak accident and not deliberate sabotage so she'd have to walk to the bank," Noah countered. "Maybe Cory was lying in wait for Jason and Linda showed up instead."

"That's possible, I suppose." Something about Noah's supposition teased the back of Shelby's mind, but she couldn't quite grasp the significance.

"I don't think Cory's our man," Cindi announced, planting herself in front of them.

"Okay. I'll bite." Noah threw up his arms. "Why not?"

"A couple of things," Cindi said slowly. "He's not paying for that car. His father gave it to him as a graduation present. His father gives him anything he wants, including money. Cory calls it guilt compensation because his dad is too busy to spend much time with him."

"He's a pretty flimsy suspect at this point," Shelby said. "Still, if he doesn't have an alibi . . ."

"He does for last night." Cindi shook her head in dismay. "He went to a beach party right after he left C.J.'s. One of his friends gave him a hard time for being late."

"Somebody knows what time he arrived?" Shelby asked.

Cindi nodded. "Twelve-fifteen. So he couldn't have robbed Linda at the bank."

"Well, that's just great." Noah seemed almost desperate. "I've tangled with Cory twice. He's not going to forget it, either. I won't be able to leave my house until he goes to college in the fall!"

"Don't worry, Noah," Shelby said. "He'll be leaving, but not for college. I think I know how to get him taken out of circulation for loan-sharking. But that's not what I'm bummed about."

Noah and Cindi exchanged bewildered glances.

Shelby clarified. "Whoever robbed Linda also robbed the tourists. Jason and Cory both have alibis. So maybe I've been wrong about this case from the start."

Cindi paled. "You don't mean . . ."

Shelby nodded. As hard as it was to believe, it looked like Will was the tourist robber after all.

Chapter
11

Nobody said much as Cindi drove back to the police station. The Saturday afternoon traffic slowed them down, making Shelby edgy. She had to act immediately if she wanted to put Cory out of the loan-sharking business. And she needed to be alone for a while to think. She couldn't shake the nagging suspicion that she had overlooked something vital in the case—something that would explain all the incriminating evidence against Will.

"I'll call you later!" Jumping out of the car, Shelby ran into the station. Detective Hineline was out, but Tracy Mendoza came in just as Shelby finished writing a note to leave on his desk. "Officer Mendoza!"

"Hi, Shelby. Are you working this afternoon?"

"No, but I've got a lead on a loan shark you might want to follow up."

"Are you poking around in something you shouldn't be again?" Tracy raised an eyebrow, but she took the paper Shelby held out.

"No, of course not." Shelby pretended to look hurt. "I just happened to overhear a conversation and thought the police should know about it."

Mendoza's dark eyes widened. "Cory *Conrad* is a loan shark? *Clayton* Conrad's son?"

Shelby nodded. "I know Mr. Conrad's a prominent citizen, but he's so involved with everything else, he doesn't spend much time with his son. Being a bully and loaning people money at outrageous interest rates is probably Cory's way of getting back at his father. But it's still illegal."

"How sure are you?" Mendoza asked cautiously.

"Very. I might even know someone who'd be willing to testify against him." She didn't want to commit Jason to a court appearance without asking him first. However, she was almost certain he'd agree.

The officer glanced at the wall clock and said, "Almost four. If I'm going to nab Cory at the pier, I'd better hustle. After the mistakes I made in the tourist robbery case, I can use a solid arrest and conviction on my record. Thanks."

"No problem." With that duty done, Shelby opened her bag to drop in her pen and saw the plastic bag. She stared at the nail that was found in Linda's tire. It matched the nails in Jason's carpenter's apron, but so did thousands of other nails in Cocoa Beach. Still, her instincts told her something about it was important. What that something was continued to elude her, though.

Sighing, Shelby closed her bag and left. She thought about stopping by the holding cells to see Will, but she just couldn't face him. He might be as guilty as the evidence indicated. If he was innocent, it meant that she had finally tackled a case she couldn't solve and she had totally let him down.

Walking home, Shelby stubbornly reviewed the details of the tourist and bank bag robberies again. But there weren't any suspects besides Will—none with a C.J.'s connection who knew what they needed to know to frame him. Stumped, her thoughts wandered back to Cory. At least, his illegal activities were about to come to an abrupt end. Then she remembered what Noah had said when he was so desperate to convince her that Cory might still be a likely suspect in the tourist robbery case.

"Well, maybe the nail in Linda's tire was just a freak accident and not deliberate sabotage so she'd have to walk to the bank," Noah countered. *"Maybe Cory was lying in wait for Jason and Linda showed up instead."*

But the nail wasn't a freak accident.

Shelby was sure of it. The fact that the nail matched Jason's nails might be a major coincidence, but it had been jammed into the *side* of the tire. And that could happen only if someone had done it deliberately.

Shelby stopped dead in her tracks, remembering something her grandfather had once told her.

Sometimes the motive for a crime isn't *what seems to be obvious.*

Deliberately puncturing a tire was a crime.

Mind racing, Shelby started walking again, faster. She had been assuming that someone had flattened Linda's tire so she'd have to walk to the bank, making it easier to snatch the bank bag.

But what if someone ruined the tire to keep Linda from going somewhere else?

Of course! Shelby stopped dead in the middle of the sidewalk and slapped her forehead. She had been thrown off the track so early in her investigation, all the obvious connections between the robber and the crimes had totally eluded her.

When Shelby considered the evidence starting from this new perspective, all the pieces clicked neatly into place. Like a line of dominos falling when the first one topples, the clues Shelby had misinterpreted or missed entirely began to make sense.

And the identity of the tourist and bank bag thief became obvious.

But she didn't have hard evidence that connected the guilty person to the crimes.

The robber planted all the evidence in Will's room. . . .

"I got the bank bag from under my bed, but I don't know how it got there." Totally bewildered, Will shook his head. "There's a bunch of other stuff that doesn't belong to me, either. I was just looking for my shoes."

Spotting Shelby, Hineline waved her inside, then handed her his handkerchief and a plastic evidence bag. "As long as you're here, make yourself useful. Look under the bed."

Under any other circumstances, Shelby would have been thrilled to be part of an official investi-

gation. But, as she carefully retrieved three wallets and three watches from under Will's bed . . .

Wallets and watches—but no cash or credit cards!

Shelby ran to the nearest pay phone. She had a good idea where to find the stolen credit cards, but she wanted backup. Cindi was home and promised to leave immediately to pick up Noah. They agreed to meet at C.J.'s. Detective Hineline was away from his desk, so she left a brief message on his voice mail: "I have a new lead in the tourist robbery case. Will didn't do it. I'll be at C.J.'s."

Since she was walking, Shelby expected to find Cindi and Noah waiting for her at the burger joint, but the blue convertible wasn't in the parking lot. Linda Alvarez's car was.

Taking care not to be seen, Shelby peeked through the front window. Linda was talking to Carmen, who usually worked during the week. The owner must have called her in to cover for Will. Shelby couldn't tell if Linda was just arriving or getting ready to leave. There was no sign of Peter.

And she was absolutely positive Peter was the tourist robber.

Still stunned because she had dismissed him as a suspect so early in the investigation, Shelby stared at Linda's car. Hineline needed permission or a search warrant to open the trunk. Otherwise, the evidence might not be admissible in court and Peter would get off on a technicality.

Shelby impulsively decided to check the trunk herself. She had to be sure the stolen credit cards were there before she told the detective. If Hineline got a warrant based on information she gave him and it turned out to be a false lead, he would be horribly humiliated. He wouldn't tolerate anything that damaged his professional reputation. He might even be mad enough to fire her.

Digging in her bag, Shelby found a long, U-shaped hairpin one of her grandfather's elderly guests had left behind. Like the flashlight, she carried it just in case circumstances arose that required one. She had never actually tried to open a lock with it before, but hairpins always worked on TV.

But they don't work in real life, Shelby realized a moment later. The pin not only failed to jimmy open the lock, it bent. And now it was stuck!

The only thing working in Will's favor was that Peter Alvarez didn't know anyone suspected him of being the tourist robber. So he might not be covering his tracks. Shelby was not about to underestimate him. Peter was smart. The difficulty she had had figuring out the clues proved that. The hairpin would alert Peter that someone had tried to get into the trunk. Warned, he'd have plenty of time to hide his stolen stash somewhere else before the police could get a warrant. Possession of the credit cards was the only means of proving Peter was guilty and Will wasn't. It was that simple.

Annoyed with her own stupidity, Shelby tugged on the bent wire. It wouldn't budge.

"What are you doing, Shelby?"

Turning at the sound of Peter's voice behind her, Shelby stood in front of the trunk lock. "Hi, Peter. I'm just waiting for my friends to—"

"Yeah, right," Peter said with a sneer. Shoving her aside, he glared at the jammed hairpin in the lock. "Think you're pretty smart, don't you?"

"I don't know what you're talking about, Peter. I was just—"

"Breaking into the trunk of my sister's car." A sly smile split Peter's tanned face as he yanked the hairpin out of the lock and handed it to her.

"Lucky for you I've got somewhere to go or I'd call the cops."

Now Shelby was certain the credit cards were in the car. Peter wanted to leave so he could get rid of them.

Frantic, Shelby blocked the way when Peter tried to push between her and the car. Somehow, she had to keep him there until Hineline or Cindi and Noah arrived. But Peter was bigger, stronger and as desperate as she was.

"Out of my way!" Grabbing Shelby's arm, Peter swung her around and pushed her down. Her head hit the bumper as she fell.

Stunned, Shelby blinked. She was looking up at the underside of the rear of the car. When she tried to sit up, her head swam and she fell back on the pavement.

Peter jumped into the car and started the engine.

Too dizzy to stand, Shelby began to crawl out of the way. In the alley ahead, Cindi's blue Ford screeched to a halt, blocking the back drive.

Shelby sized up the situation in a split second.

Peter's only way out of the parking lot was backward toward the main street.

And she was lying directly in the path of the tires. . . .

Chapter
12

Certain that her life was about to come to a sudden and crushing end in C.J.'s parking lot, Shelby struggled to her hands and knees.

Cindi and Noah ran toward the car, waving and shouting at Peter. "Wait! Don't—"

The engine roared as Peter put his foot on the gas and shifted into reverse.

The wheels spun.

A silent scream of frightened outrage echoed in Shelby's mind as she frantically scrambled for safety. *I'm not gonna make it!*

A powerful hand clamped around Shelby's arm and yanked her clear as the car suddenly sped backward.

Dazed by the close call, Shelby looked up at Detective Hineline's pale face. Both of their heads snapped around as the screech of worn brakes broke the terrified tension that gripped them.

Peter stopped his sister's car within inches of ramming a police cruiser blocking the exit into the street. Flashing a badge, an officer pulled Peter out of the car.

"Shelby! Are you okay?" Cindi called breathlessly as she and Noah ran up.

Shelby nodded and glanced at the shaken detective. "Yeah, thanks to Detective Hineline. That was close."

"Too close." Hineline scowled.

"I think the stolen credit cards are in the trunk of that car," Shelby said quickly, hoping to divert the detective's attention from her narrow escape.

"What's going on?" Linda raced out of the restaurant and stopped short when she saw the officer clamping handcuffs on her younger brother. "Is Peter in trouble?"

"I'm afraid so, Ms. Alvarez," Hineline said. "We have probable cause that allows us to legally search your car—"

Linda's eyes flashed defensively. "You need a warrant!"

"Not when someone almost runs over an innocent bystander trying to evade the police, ma'am." Hineline looked at the troubled young woman levelly. "We can use a crowbar or you can give me the keys."

Shoulders sagging, Linda nodded.

"Does this mean Will is innocent?" Cindi whispered as Linda took the keys out of the ignition. Hineline gave them to the uniformed officer.

"We'll know in a minute." Shelby hardly dared breathe as she watched the officer remove the piles of junk stored in the trunk.

"Looks like we hit the jackpot, sir!" Grinning, the officer held up a plastic bag full of credit cards and money. "It was in the spare tire compartment."

Laughing, Cindi jumped up and down with excitement.

Noah slapped Shelby on the back.

Shelby heaved a huge sigh of relief. Not only had she proven that Will was innocent, her crime-solving record was still perfect.

* * *

Later, sitting around a table at C.J.'s, Shelby and her friends held their final case conference. As usual at eight o'clock on a Saturday night, business was booming.

"I've spent the past half hour trying to figure out how you figured out Peter was guilty," Cindi said, squeezing ketchup over her fries. "I don't have a clue."

"Me, neither." Noah snatched a fry and popped it in his mouth. "The only thing I've figured out is that most of Peter's odd jobs involved stealing from someone. So give."

"Well, Noah"—Shelby leaned forward, her dark eyes sparkling—"you actually gave me the hint I needed."

"I did?" Noah sat up straighter.

"Yes." Shelby nodded emphatically. "Peter didn't flatten Linda's tire because he wanted his sister to walk to the bank. He wanted to delay her from getting *home*. Once I knew that, I realized that he had done the same thing the nights of the tourist robberies using a different tactic."

The first time Linda dropped a clue was at C.J.'s the afternoon Peter was going to help Jason on a remodeling job and had to borrow Linda's car.

Linda gave the car keys to Peter.

"Thanks, Linda. I'll be back at nine to pick you up."

"Don't be late. And make sure the gas tank's not empty, okay?" Linda eyed him sternly.

The second time she mentioned gas was last night when we were staking out C.J.'s and Peter brought the car back again.

"The car's parked in the side lot, Linda." Peter stopped his sister on her way back to the door.

Linda took the car keys Peter held out and stuffed them in her jeans pocket. "Do I have enough gas to get home?"

"I filled it up. Gotta run."

When Detective Hineline and I drove Linda home after she had been robbed at the bank, she confirmed that Peter usually returned the car with an empty tank.

Collapsing on the sofa, Linda began to cry softly. "Sometimes you just can't win. Peter finally remembers to put gas in the car so I won't have to stop on my way home like I have been on Fridays and what happens? I get a flat tire. I have to walk to the bank and—somebody robs me!"

Linda was getting annoyed with having to put gas in the car every Friday night. So Peter used a nail he took from Jason's carpenter's apron on the remodeling job to give her a flat tire instead.

"What for?" Cindi asked.

Shelby sat back. "So Linda wouldn't know what time he *really* got home. She might have gotten suspicious."

Noah threw up his hands. "That's right! Cindi and I should have made that connection after we talked to Mr. MacDougal."

Shelby nodded.

I didn't realize the significance when you told me about it at C.J.'s later, either.

The man was getting nervous and seemed anxious to defend his dog.

"He's barking at us now," Noah said. "Doesn't he bark at the neighbors? If they come home late or something?"

"No. That new woman across the street drove in while we were outside last night and Caesar didn't make a peep!"

"After twelve-fifteen?" Cindi asked excitedly.

"More like twelve-twenty-five, I'd say. About five minutes after her brother finished running. Caesar didn't bark at him, either."

"Her brother goes running after midnight?" Noah asked.

Mr. MacDougal rolled his eyes. *"That kid runs all the time. He must go around this block a hundred times a day. And he always carries a wooden stick, like he's training for some race or something."*

Peter was running a race all right. He had to beat his sister home after he committed the robberies.

"And Peter could run fast enough to do it, too!" Cindi nodded. "He's got all those track trophies to prove it."

"But why would he risk hurting his own sister by robbing her?" Noah scratched his head.

"You pegged that one, too, Noah," Shelby said. "He was expecting *Jason* to show up at the bank. With her hair tied back and most of the overhead lights burned out, Linda looked like Jason from behind in the dark."

Peter didn't know he had stolen the bank bag from Linda until Detective Hineline and I took her home.

Peter was lounging on the sofa watching TV. He kept his eyes on the screen as he casually flipped through the channels. "Hi, Sis. What took you so long?"

"I, uh—was robbed. At the bank."

The remote dropped from Peter's hand as he sat up and stared at Linda. The blood drained from his face. "You were—"

"Don't worry," Linda said quickly. "I'm all right. Detective Hineline and Shelby were driving by—"

Peter's head snapped around. "They saw it happen?"

"I'm afraid not," Hineline said. "The thief was gone when we arrived."

Nodding, Peter jumped up and rushed to help Linda to the couch.

He was really worried that he might have hurt her.

"But he wasn't worried that anyone would discover the stash in the trunk of the car," Shelby continued. "He knew Linda wouldn't want to spend money on a service call. And he really didn't want to get a ride back to the car with Detective Hineline, either. The bank bag was in his backpack, but he couldn't refuse without arousing Hineline's suspicions."

"That guy has nerves of steel," Noah observed.

"And he thinks quickly in a crisis," Shelby added.

I wanted to search the car because I thought Linda might have faked the robbery. I gave up that idea when I found the gas receipt that proved she had an alibi for the third tourist robbery.

Leaning on the rear fender, Shelby held the flashlight beam on the flat tire. She glanced at the backpack lying on a pile of old magazines, dirty rags, empty oil containers and assorted auto parts in the trunk. "Want me to get your other tools?"

Ignoring the question, Peter sat back on his heels. "Would you look at that!"

"What?" Curious, Shelby squatted to look.

"This!" Peter pointed to a huge nail in the

sidewall of the tire. "Linda couldn't have picked it up on the street, Shelby. Someone jammed this into her tire on purpose."

Peter realized he could throw suspicion onto someone else by pointing out the nail. But he also used it to distract me so I wouldn't see his stolen stash in the spare tire compartment. . . .

"Okay." Cindi frowned thoughtfully. "All of that makes sense. But why frame Will? Why not frame a total stranger?"

Shelby wrinkled her nose sheepishly. "That's my fault, actually."

Peter overheard me talking to Will at C.J.'s. . . .

Shelby smiled. "Don't worry, okay? Just because the police think you're the tourist robber . . ." The rest of her words trailed off as Noah deliberately spilled the basket of fries on the floor and ducked under the table with Cindi. ". . . doesn't mean that we do."

"I'm not worried." Will peered under the

table. "Do you want to eat them off the floor or should I clean them up?"

Noah and Cindi frantically waved him away.

Out of the corner of her eye, Shelby saw Linda and Peter Alvarez walking to the counter. She was worried that they had overheard what she said to Will. Since no charges had been filed, no one except the police, herself and her friends knew that Will was the primary suspect in the tourist robbery case. A rumor like that could be all over town within a few hours.

I'm afraid that gave Peter the idea. And he didn't waste any time putting his plan into action.

"Linda told Jason I was handy with a hammer, so he offered me a couple hours' work on a remodeling job," Peter explained. "I want to write down the address before I forget it."

"Sure!" Always eager to please, Will gave him the C.J.'s pen tucked over his left ear.

Peter scribbled on the back of a paper napkin, then shoved the napkin and the pen into his pocket.

Peter was wearing work gloves, so his prints weren't on the pen. When he deliberately dropped it at the bank, he knew the police would find Will's fingerprints and no one else's.

Shelby picked up a fry and paused a moment to eat it. "Peter figured the police would get a search warrant based on the pen. He called Will, disguising his voice and pretending to be Linda after he fixed the tire and drove me home. He assumed that Will was *so* infatuated with his sister, he wouldn't wonder too much because her voice sounded funny. And he was right. Will fell for it hook, line and sinker. When Will left the house, Peter planted the wallets and watches under his bed."

Noah nodded. "So the police would find all the evidence they needed for an arrest."

"Right." Shelby slumped slightly. "But everyone missed the most obvious clue. I didn't give it a thought until after I had everything else figured out."

"What clue is that?" Cindi started.

"The weapon the robber used to scare those poor tourists into cooperating."

Cindi and Noah looked at each other, then fixed Shelby with blank stares.

"So what was it?" Noah asked finally.

"Peter's practice relay baton. He always carried his backpack and the wooden dowel was always in it."

Cindi and Noah both groaned, glanced at the ceiling, then buried their faces in their hands. They looked up as the door flew open. His expression totally miserable, Will shuffled to their table.

"What's the matter?" Cindi asked anxiously.

"Linda quit. She said she couldn't keep working at the scene of Peter's crimes. And she's got to find a better job to pay his legal expenses." Sighing, Will hung his head. "I'll probably never see her again."

Noah rolled his eyes. "That's no loss, Will. Her brother tried to frame you for robbery!"

"So?"

"So—aren't you glad you're out of jail?" Cindi asked.

"Yeah." Will nodded and graced Shelby with a quick smile before his depressed frown returned. "Thanks for getting me out of there, Shelby."

"You're welcome." Shelby beamed with pride,

then shifted uncomfortably. She loved tackling difficult mysteries and solving them, but she didn't expect excessive gratitude from the innocent people she helped. Knowing that the guilty would pay for their crimes was reward enough. Then again, being appreciated for her brilliant efforts was nice, too.

"Being in jail was the pits, but it got a lot worse real fast when they put Cory Conrad in the cell next to me."

"Cory's in jail?" Noah's face brightened.

Shelby grinned. Apparently, Officer Mendoza had gotten to the pier in time to catch Cory accepting money from another victim.

"Yeah, he's in the slammer. Listening to Cory complain was almost as bad as the food." Sighing heavily again, Will muttered as he wandered to the counter. "Maybe I'll make myself a burger or two before I clock in."

"Well, losing the love of his life hasn't affected Will's appetite." Cindi shook her head.

"A little more gratitude would be nice, though," Noah said with a grin. "If it wasn't for Shelby, he'd be eating prison food for a *long* time."

Case closed, Shelby thought with a satisfied smile.

*   *   *

Shelby clicked open her personal computer file on the tourist robbery case to make her final entry.

Jason Hopkins has agreed to testify against Cory. Overall, things have turned out pretty well for the artist. He quit his job at C.J.'s because an interior decorator commissioned several paintings for the yacht club lobby. And because he sold almost everything at the Cocoa Beach Sidewalk Art Show, he has to paint like crazy. Otherwise he won't have anything to display at his one-man show in Palm Beach. Would you believe he invited me to the opening reception? I can't wait. . . .

"Shelby!" Detective Hineline hollered. "There's a smudge on my badge!"

Shelby looked up to see the metal shield sailing through the air. She caught it with one hand, rubbed it on her shirt, tossed it back and resumed typing.

C.J.'s is back to normal, too—except for Will. Everyone, myself included, is hoping he gets over his broken heart and stops crying about Linda soon. We're all getting really tired of eating soggy hamburger buns.

About the Author

Diana G. Gallagher lives in Minnesota with her husband, Marty Burke, three dogs, three cats, and a cranky parrot. When she's not writing, she likes to read, walk the dogs and look for cool stuff at garage sales for her grandsons, Jonathon and Alan.

Diana and Marty are musicians who perform traditional and original Irish and American folk music at coffeehouses and conventions around the country. Marty sings and plays the twelve-string guitar and banjo. In addition to singing backup harmonies, Diana plays rhythm guitar and a round, Celtic drum called a *bodhran*.

A Hugo Award–winning artist, Diana is best known for her series *Woof: The House Dragon*. Her first adult novel, *The Alien Dark*, appeared in 1990. She and Marty coauthored *The Chance Factor*, a STAR-FLEET ACADEMY VOYAGER book. In addition to other STAR TREK novels for intermediate readers, Diana has written many books in other series published by Minstrel Books, including *The Secret World of Alex Mack*, *Are You Afraid of the Dark?*, and *The Mystery Files of Shelby Woo*. She is currently working on original young adult novels for the Archway Paperback series *Sabrina, the Teenage Witch*.

GO BEYOND THE BOOKS AND ENTER THE WORLD OF

Bruce Coville's **MY TEACHER** is an **ALIEN**

CD-ROM GAME

You've always suspected that your teacher is an alien... But no one believed you. Now, to save your life, you have one week to prove it.

In this action-adventure CD-ROM game for fans of Bruce Coville's *My Teacher* book series, you'll encounter high-speed action sequences and mind-bending puzzles. You choose to play as one of the main characters—Susan, Peter, or Duncan—to help them foil the alien's evil plot. Your every move determines how the game will end— you'll have to think fast and act even faster to stop the alien before time runs out.

Available November 1997 $34.95 Windows® 95 CD-ROM

To order, call
1-888-793-9973
Promo key: 440255 • Product number: 401174

http://www.byronpreiss.com

 SIMON & SCHUSTER INTERACTIVE

#1 THE TALE OF THE SINISTER STATUES 52545-X/$3.99

#2 THE TALE OF CUTTER'S TREASURE 52729-0/$3.99

#3 THE TALE OF THE RESTLESS HOUSE 52547-6/$3.99

#4 THE TALE OF THE NIGHTLY NEIGHBORS 53445-9/$3.99

#5 THE TALE OF THE SECRET MIRROR 53671-0/$3.99

#6 THE TALE OF THE PHANTOM SCHOOL BUS 53672-9/$3.99

#7 THE TALE OF THE GHOST RIDERS 56252-5/$3.99

#8 THE TALE OF THE DEADLY DIARY 53673-7/$3.99

#9 THE TALE OF THE VIRTUAL NIGHTMARE 00080-2/$3.99

#10 THE TALE OF THE CURIOUS CAT 00081-0/$3.99

#11 THE TALE OF THE ZERO HERO 00357-7/$3.99

#12 THE TALE OF THE SHIMMERING SHELL 00392-5/$3.99

#13 THE TALE OF THE THREE WISHES 00358-5/$3.99

#14 THE TALE OF THE CAMPFIRE VAMPIRES 00908-7/$3.99

A MINSTREL BOOK

Simon & Schuster Mail Order Dept. BWB
200 Old Tappan Rd., Old Tappan, N.J. 07675

Please send me the books I have checked above. I am enclosing $_____(please add $0.75 to cover the postage and handling for each order. Please add appropriate sales tax). Send check or money order--no cash or C.O.D.'s please. Allow up to six weeks for delivery. For purchase over $10.00 you may use VISA: card number, expiration date and customer signature must be included.

Name _____

Address _____

City _____ State/Zip _____

VISA Card # _____ Exp.Date _____

Signature _____ 1053-13